From A to Zoe
A Novel

MARIE-JO FORTIS

Published by LIBURU PRESS
244 5th Avenue, Suite F-217
New York, NY 10001

ISBN: 0692399437
ISBN 13: 9780692399439

This book is for all women.

All ages.

All colors.

All crying, all laughing. All falling, all rising.

All women.

With a special thought for women facing cancer.

ZOE

Means "life" in Greek. From early times it was adopted by Hellenized Jews as a translation of EVE.

www.behindthename.com/name/zoe

Je t'aime je t'aime
Oh oui je t'aime
Moi non plus

Serge Gainsbourg

Note from the author: When stereotactic breast biopsy is explained in chapter 4 (mostly by character Dr. Fontaine), I have taken the liberty of using some of the language I read in a brochure on the procedure from the Northwest Medical Center in Oil City, the place where I underwent my own stereotactic breast biopsy.

PROLOGUE

Five months in New York City. Five months plus twelve days, to be precise. In lieu of the Big Apple, right now I would much prefer a more sizable one, a red delicious, if possible.

■ ■ ■

So here I am. Away from the small Pennsylvania town of Noliar and the maple-and-oak jungle that surrounds it. With the help of a New Yorker friend—you know, the type who thinks there is no life outside of bumper-to-bumper traffic, theater, and skyscrapers; with the help of that friend who, for lack of imagination, always confuses *bucolic* with *idiotic*, I got a place. Not much of a place, mind you, but it's rent controlled with utilities and cranky home phone included on Seventy-Second Street, not far from the statue of the great Eleanor Roosevelt. Not that I care. If you're one of those feminists looking at these pages, don't stop breathing yet. It's not that I dislike good old Ms. Roosevelt. I admire Eleanor and her cousin of a husband. I just don't like statues. One reason is that they don't move. There is another reason I don't like statues: you know what the birds do to them after a meal of worms because they can't move.

My name is Zoe Zimmerman. Some friends call me Zoe; some friends call me Z-Z. My parents like the last letter of the alphabet, I guess. They named my brother Ziegfried. Siegfried sounded too heroic, they said, too hard to bear. And they thought *Ziegfried* would be easier? Mind you, if there's one person who deserves a silly name, it's my brother. That said, silliness is to be expected when your mother is Catholic and your father is Jewish. That fact alone gave me so many headaches that I almost became a Buddhist. Of course, the statues were the deal breaker. There's no way birds are more polite with a sitting Buddha than they are with a standing Eleanor.

Writing is my religion. Writing and reading, actually. It's what I've been doing since I was eight years old. Although, if you ask me, that sounds a bit redundant. Writing and reading are pretty much the same thing. "You say that, and you call *me* stupid?" my brother Zieg said once with a voice like a trombone. When we were in high school, the marching band lost one of theirs, and I offered them a perfect solution: let my brother march with them and have him sing. That would do the trick. Of course, they never took my proposal seriously. Had he lived in a big city, he might be famous right now. As it is, he's a computer specialist. Was on the verge of becoming an accountant before that. He nixed the idea of accounting when he decided that the jargon—schedule A or form 1040, form 2106 or schedule C, E-Z, and so forth—might deaden his wit. Yeah, OK. Like he's the life of the party now, with his poetic lexicon comprised of such beauties as *International Data Encryption Algorithm*—IDEA for short; how brilliant. Or *Motorola 680x0*. This one sounds sexy: *pipeline burst cache*—it should be included in *The Dictionary of Porn for Idiots*.

Besides the Z in our names, the only thing Zieg and I have in common is the red mane. It's a big mass and a big mess. But people burst out in orgasmic oohs and aahs when they see all that red hair. Zieg keeps his short now. I've kept mine long, for charity's sake. Any kind of orgasm I can offer to others is fine with me. I must check with the IRS to see if it's tax deductible.

I digress, sure, but digression is what a writer does for a living. Not that I'm making much of a living as a writer. I mean, look at my place. Let's see, how to describe it in one word? *Mm.* Minimalist. Minimalist in size, minimalist hygiene-wise. The kitchen, living room, and bedroom are spread over a glorious space of fourteen feet by ten feet. A closet in its former life, the bathroom trumpets its glory with a toilet that could wake a deaf regiment. There is no way a friend can tell me she's just going to powder her nose with a system like this.

I share my palace with Ziegfried II. We had to get used to each other, and it didn't take that long. Each night, he would come and cross the place at all speed, stop for a minute, look at me, mustache shivering and all, then cross the room again and hide. I started leaving a piece of Swiss cheese by his observation post. The first night he saw it, he looked at it, danced around it, smelled it, and left without even giving me a glance. I thought, too bad, buddy, you don't want it, see if I care, I am going to bed. When I woke up, the cheese was gone. So the following night, I pretty much did the same thing. Little Ziegfrid II arrived on schedule, grabbed the cheese, and left in a hurry. On the third night, he was kind enough to say good-bye—he gave me a glimpse and a twitch of the nose and was off. After a week, we were having our dinners together, he under the limping chair (a.k.a. *the antique*) and I on the sofa (a.k.a. *the cogitating corner*, now retired from its former function as a giant napkin for preschoolers or a palette for budding artists).

The furniture also includes a Formica table having gone through the Ajax-manias (or was it Bon Ami, mon ami?) of self-fulfilled housewives (a species now defunct) and a dresser whose first and third drawers are bottomless. These ritzy furnishings came with the place. I can't complain, it's Manhattan!

Maybe I'll stay in this place another month or two.

Maybe I'll start again. If I do, Ziegfried II won't mind, and I guess I won't, either, even though the damn rat won't pay rent. From the way this little guy picks up his cheese with his two little arms, and nibbles on it like some duchess at tea time, I know he's got better table manners than some acquaintances of mine.

1

I am carefully folding sheets of paper. Many publishers and agents accept submissions the e-way, but some still insist on snail mail. And, let's face it, I am desperate to use my tongue, even if only for licking envelopes.

Early in the morning, the sky had on its gray, grouchy dress, to match the mood of New Yorkers. But now, it looks like a giant eraser is removing the gloom. Through the deletions here and there, I can see some yellowish patches, diverse facets of the shy winter sun. I twist a chunk of hair with my finger, and I see the trembling light painting several shades of red on it. I want to bathe in the hesitant warmth, call it, say it's OK to be warmer still. I want to let the sun know that I have had it with its seasonal bashfulness. But I suppose I have to wait.

Looking out the broken window—hastily repaired with masking tape, and only reminiscent of a mosaic if you have a lot of imagination—I can make out a few things outside. Granted, it is a broken, cubic perspective. Still, I know. I know from glancing at the silhouettes awkwardly progressing from within their fortresses of thick coats and hats and scarves, and at the merchants hurriedly positioning their stalls of fruit and flowers on the sidewalk. And, from the sight of Mr. Berlusconi rubbing his arms while chatting with the early-rising retirees from the doorstep of his tobacco shop, I know damn well it's no more than fifteen degrees outside. I don't need to see the head of the man right under my eyes to know it belongs to

Jack Liu, the neighborhood florist. Jack may have the most beautiful roses in the city, but he's got no taste in hats. His is a faux Davy Crockett without the tail. So all the necessary clues are here. Winter is here. But I don't need to look. When you're wearing two pairs of socks, flannel pajamas, and an imitation wool robe made in China, you know you're not in Rio de Janeiro or any kind of cha-cha land.

Still, I am hungry for the outside. Hungry to do anything but stuffing envelopes with my latest masterpiece.

Yet, I start licking the butt of the envelopes with all my love. I pretend the glue that will seal my pages and my fate tastes like a nice glass of merlot. It takes all the imagination I can muster, but, I tell myself, dammit, I am a novelist. After all, if I want, I can create a brainless US president and send him to Mars in quest of hallucinogenic mushrooms, hoping these will give him the gray cells he seems to have lost somewhere between birth and Timbuktu.

■ ■ ■

I contemplate my envelopes, now sealed in proper fashion. After considerable licking, the merlot thing stops working as a suspension of disbelief, and the bitter taste of the glue returns with a vengeance. I have bought three books of stamps representing animals of the jungle, and I thank the patron saint of the USPS for having made them self-sticking.

For years I have made love to words. Some were in dire need of Cialis, so I sent them away and called back others. I am a gardener pruning the dead weight. I am a musician looking for the right rhythm. I am the Cuisinart mixing up the traits of friends and foes to invent new characters who, coincidentally, will remind the reader of Grandma Georgette, who always gets Christmas presents for her grandkids at the Salvation Army or from one of her mothballed closets; or visually impaired Uncle Terrence, who crochets hats, scarves, and shawls with holes bigger than the Grand Canyon. I am the scribe of these eccentrics, believe it or not, and if the idea ever comes to me to change a few things without asking their advice, boy, am I screwed! Patricia the Prude or Martin the Accountant hits me on the head and screams, "Where the hell did that shit come from?"

My characters can be a real pain, but there is an upside to that. I can actually be a murderer and get away with it. If, for instance, Ed Esophagus-Ignoramus too often speaks with his mouth full, I can send him to the precipice, to the overdose, or to his mother-in-law, Bernice.

We really are a dysfunctional family, my characters and I. I can't live with them, can't live without them. Yet, I anticipate my liberation. It comes when the novel is finished, I'm sure of it. At that point, it's bye-bye, boogers. Freedom, yoo-hoo! Yoo-hoo? Wait. I need to do one more thing: I type *the end*. The end. I have reached it. You would think I could breathe at last. But no, something else happens. My face gets wet. I cry like a baby. It's not good-bye and good riddance. It's *bonjour, tristesse*, dammit. I have been drained. But what I feel now is not the fatigue. It's the void.

■ ■ ■

I light a candle next to the envelopes. Do literary agents have a patron saint? My mom knows the whole array of them, in alphabetical order. My dad mumbles between his teeth that Catholics are a bunch of pagans. "Like you Torah readers have it all together," my mom replies. "Like Moses really opened up the Red Sea with a stick."

"Very possible," my dad says. "Moses was a stutterer. He might have stuttered with his damn stick as well. The sea might have been in disagreement as to what he meant and parted ways."

"You don't believe in anything, not even in your damn religion," my mom says.

"I'll have you know that Moses is part of your Bible as well." My father smiles, thinking he has won the argument. But that's counting out Mom's plots for revenge, which will come a few days later with daily servings of pork, including blood sausage, and the making of a splendid cheesecake, which my dad looks at with lusty anticipation…until he bites into it, runs to the kitchen sink, and spits. The cake is as salty and as spicy as a Polish sausage. The tricks are always the same, yet they work every time. Believe it or not, the whole process is foreplay as seen by a Catholic faux bigot and a Jew who thinks everything is kosher as long as it leads to sex. A noisy siesta always follows. According to the "notes" my brother and I have gathered and compared after several sessions of listening behind doors, both of our parents are pretty athletic, body-wise and lung-wise. After every siesta, Mom thanks St. Rita of Cascia, the patron saint of challenging marriages, which only triggers Dad's mockeries. And so it starts again.

Right now, though, I decide to be practical and side with Mom. I need all the help I can get to find me an agent. From my mother's indefatigable enumerations, I seem to recall that St. François de Sales, a sixteenth-century French guy, is the patron saint of writers. So I ask the venerable Francis to help me make it.

That's my version of suspension of disbelief.

I place the envelopes in a plastic bag and put a coat on over my pajamas. I add a hat, scarf, and gloves, and I am grateful that they were made by some machine in China and not crocheted by Uncle Terrence. I pick up the bag, give it a last blessing, and I'm off to the mailbox.

Before I leave, I hear him get up.

Why did I let him in, when I had promised myself this would never, ever happen again?

And how did he find me?

2

When I come back, I hear it all.

The clank is formidable. The world conference of carpenters at Niagara Falls. It invades the whole place and interrupts my daydream. That damn toilet! I have talked to the super about installing a new one with a more discreet flush, but the man, lips and beer belly moving in rhythm, his piggy eyes traveling from my breasts to my feet and back, declares, "Hey lady, it works, don't it? Does its job pretty darn good, eh?" And then, from a liver mouth adorned with a brown tooth here and there, he emits a laugh full of bacon, sausage, and butter. "Those new c'modes, they don't flush like that no more. I tell ya, I don't know where the world's goin' with those little mousy flushes that don't take all they're s'pose to take."

■ ■ ■

"Have you thought about talking to the super about the toilet?" he asks, his voice a caressing baritone.

If Samantha from *Bewitched* had decided to create a WASP out of Che Guevara at the first twitch of her nose, Marc would have been the end result. Gorgeous, neat, his beard trimmed like a lawn in Beverly Hills, tall, handsome, muscular—he's your perfect Harlequin romance guy. Only in the early hours does he stand unchecked.

Like now. This is when he looks his best, in the morning, his curly black hair disheveled, his deep-blue eyes without glasses, naked, full of myopia and mystery and the remnants of a dream. Full of tenderness, too. Nearsighted people have very romantic eyes, my pothead friend told me. She was fixing my myopic gaze when she said that. And I thought the girl had had too much dope. But now I understand, looking at vulnerable, beautiful Marc.

"No," I lie.

"Why?"

"Well, I hear the man is gorgeous. A Socratic mind, on top of that. I wouldn't want to be tempted. Or you to be jealous."

He approaches, sits on the floor besides me, starts brushing warm kisses on my neck.

"You shouldn't," I say.

"Why?" he murmurs between kisses.

I feel his beard on the top of my back, his hands removing my robe. "Take off your glasses," he whispers.

"I can't see without my glasses."

"Neither can I. It doesn't matter. Please."

"No."

"What's the matter? You're cranky this morning."

"PMS."

"I don't think so."

"Like you would know."

"I am a doctor."

"You're not *my* doctor."

"I'm still a gynecologist. Not to mention your lover of the past two years. So tell me, Zoe, what's the matter?"

It's hard to remove myself from the gentleness of his hold, from his hands that, almost without my knowledge, have undone the buttons of my pajamas. I want him to love me now, on the floor. I want last night to start again. When I free myself, I see surprise, and a touch of sadness drifting like a current, like impressionist touches, on his still-sleepy face. I get up and walk across the room and back. It's a performance that I want to appear grand and Napoleonic, but taking one step ahead or two steps back, I am in danger of hitting the wall either way. "How did you find me?" I ask after my version of a battlefield march.

He rises, starts to come toward me, but I scream. "Marc, *stop!*"

For a moment he stands paralyzed. "What..."

"You almost stepped on Ziegfried II!"

3

"What the hell..."

"That's Ziegfried II, my companion."

Marc looks somewhat nauseated. "A rat?"

"Your point? My brother deals with mice. A mechanical mouse here, an optical mouse there. Sometimes it's only a mouse elbow, and sometimes it's a mouse port, imagine! So why can't I have a rat?"

"You should kill it. Rats spread disease."

I give Marc my meanest glance, the one catalogued as "Pissed-Off-Big-Time No. 5." A classic, like Chanel No. 5. He looks surprised, as if the glance went to the wrong target.

"Don't make such an innocent face. And don't look at me as if I were a New York cop. You didn't answer me, dammit!"

"Well, we were interrupted by your *imperial* friend, Ziegfried II."

"Marc, please!"

I try to avoid looking at his face—his beautiful Che Guevara face with the cloudy sky in his eyes and the cute bump on his nose. The waves of his beard and mustache hide his Harlequin-hero mouth. I know the man can be as delicious as a forbidden fruit. I know the perfect asylum of his arms. I know it's too good to be true.

He sits on the floor, his back against the sofa. "Zoe, look at me!"

Since I am still standing, now would be a good time to look down on him. Instead I lift my gaze to the cracked ceiling. "No!"

"Well, at least come sit with me."

Oh, God, it's hard to resist. At this point, I am not giving up. Call me a heroine for now. A postmodern Joan of Arc.

"If you come closer to me, I'll tell you."

"Tell me what!"

"How I found you."

This I need to know. And when he extends his hand toward me, I take it. For an instant I feel its warmth, and for one moment, one not-brief-enough moment, I look at it, the wide palm, the long precise fingers, the dark hair which, when brushed on my body, gives me shivers of pleasure. He draws me down, kisses me, and pulls out the pajama top that I forgot to rebutton. Joan of Arc has gone on vacation. And then his mouth is on my breasts, his lips teasing my nipples. The man is colonizing me, and I am in no insurgent mode. And then his mouth promenades, oh so slowly, down my stomach. And then his hands reenter the stage, untying my pajama bottoms and sliding them down my thighs. And then it's the mouth's turn again. And then I don't exist. And then I invade the sky, the stars, the galaxy, the universe. We are both a burn and a delight. And then I say, "Damn you!"

"Zoe, darling…"

"You tricked me!"

His hands are on my right breast; he stays silent. I remove his hands; he puts them back. I remove them again. He says, "Hold on!" His hands are moving around my nipples, then drawing larger and larger circles, and then reversing their trajectory. He's on his knees now, bending over me with something hanging. I'm about to giggle at the sight but something stops me. A sensation.

"You're hurting me!"

"Where, right here?" His fingers are pressing my breast's northeast side.

"Yes! This is not sensual, Marc. Take your hand away!"

"You have a lump," he says.

"Lumpy-bumpy, that's me!"

"This is different."

"How do you know?"

Now his glance is no longer the shade of sapphire. It's the sky in November. Shit! This means trouble.

"I'm a doctor, dammit!"

"You're not my doctor!"

"Haven't we already had that conversation?"

"I like tautology."

"Zoe, this is no joke. How come you haven't noticed this before?"

Now it's my turn to be silent.

"When was the last time you examined your breasts?"

Silence again. I like tautology there, too.

"You never listen, do you? Not to your doctor; not to me, your lover."

"You're not my lover!"

"Oh, no? And what did we do just now? Do you call that a business meeting? In this case, you're not wearing the right clothes, are you? As a matter of fact, you are not wearing any clothes at all."

Well, I have news for him. He's not wearing any clothes, either! But that doesn't prevent him from walking indignantly across the room to reach the phone.

I run to him just as he is about to pick up the receiver. I stop him. "What are you doing?"

"Calling the hospital."

"Please, don't!"

"Zoe, you need a mammogram."

"I can't have a mammogram."

"Why not?"

"I can't pay for it. I have no insurance."

He raises his eyebrows.

"OK," I add. "I've got a shitty insurance. Same difference. This damn country won't even protect its own people."

"Don't start with this." He looks at me as if I were an annoying insect. I am starting to get nostalgia for the look he had for Ziegfried II. It was kinder. I go to the couch, lock my hands around my body. Call it a fetal position if you want. I call it self-burial. A big mass of lead has fallen on my head. Only the tears raining down my face and neck tell me I am still living.

The phone is now at rest. I just heard the click, very faintly, like the closure of some secret.

■ ■ ■

"You have a mammography tomorrow at eight. Maybe an ultrasound. And then, we're going to see Dr. Fontaine."

His voice sounds cavernous, almost ominous, and far, far away. I feel I have heard it before, long time ago. It's not real. It seems it's directed to the wall on the opposite side of the room. I let the top of my head emerge from my arms and see that this is indeed the case. I see his long muscular mass, his strong legs, dancer's buttocks and back. I see his rebellious curls. The wall sees the rest of him, including his face. I feel ambivalent. What to do now? Drown in tears or laugh? Is there a possibility I could do both at once?

In the next second, the ambiguity subsides. Somehow, I have fallen from the couch, right on my ass. He forgets his conversation with the wall for now, rushes to me, and takes me into his arms. His breath in my ear feels like a tropical breeze. He whispers, "I love you, darling. I will always be with you, somehow." I shiver. He helps me put on my robe. Maybe that's not what I want now. He takes me by the arm. We walk to the bathroom. He starts the shower and then removes my robe again. He's treating me like a little girl. But I am drowsy, I do not say anything. He'll get it later, I figure, when the drowsiness subsides. Like an automaton, I let myself be guided under the shower. He joins me. He's not treating me like a little girl after all. The drowsiness lingers, but it's not the same kind as before. And I don't want to wake up.

4

Dr. Raymond Fontaine is tall and a tad plump. His ancient baby blues, faded like overwashed curtains, stick out like old planets. Yet there is something seductive about him. Like a well-practiced playboy, he shakes my hand and looks deeply into my eyes, and then looks a bit lower to see if they are fake. I figure he's in his sixties. It is clear that he wants people to think he's at least twenty years younger, what with his hair died a shade too dark and his cheeks plumped with fat from his liposuctioned butt.

With its plush carpeting and furniture with lines so pure that Brancusi himself would have felt sick with envy, Fontaine's office is that of a doctor for socialites—a doctor I cannot afford. But no matter, he will not charge one of his former star pupils, who is sitting next to me, smiling at his mentor and holding my hand as if I were the little wife and not the fucked-up mistress. Dr. Fontaine shoots an amused glance of complicity at his protégé; a glance tinted with a note of approval, it seems to say, "Well done, Marc. Your taste in women is very respectable indeed. Of course, I wouldn't expect anything less of you, as you were trained with a master, not only of gynecology, but of affairs with beautiful interns."

Or perhaps my imagination is reading too much into what was merely a glance. Perhaps that special look might have merely said, "Oh, how I would kill for caviar on toast right now!" But the old playboy collects mistresses, I can tell. And in a sense I am amazed that his profession did not make him look the other way. How a male gynecologist, who sees thirty vaginas a day, does not turn gay after a few years is beyond me. I tell Marc this time and again, only to get chuckles as an answer.

Now Dr. Fontaine picks up his designer glasses and examines the mammographies taken just this morning. Ah, the convenience of having a doctor as a lover. This does not prevent me from feeling like hell because, in order to get a mammography so soon, the hospital has probably postponed exams that were scheduled ahead of time. Maybe I have taken the place of an old lady with needs more urgent than mine.

"How do you know?" Marc said when I raised my concerns to him. "To me, your needs are the most urgent."

How sweet, I thought. Though maybe he also needs to show me how powerful he is.

Dr. Fontaine rises, sticks the mammograms up on a lighted board to the right of his desk, and invites Marc to examine them with him. I think, "Those are my boobs, dammit! Can't I be invited to look at them, too?" Marc rises, and for a while all I hear is, "Mmm...I see...do you think that...no...well...mm...OK...she...there...mmm...ahem...mm... mm..." I am faced with a choice: answer all those "Mm-mms" with "Moo, moo!" or go to the bookstore across the street and buy two copies of *A New Guide to Better Elocution.*

Instead, I look at the Marcel Pavie painting on the wall. Next to it is a Roy Lichtenstein. I definitely prefer Pavie's expressionism, his warm colors, and this, despite the subject: a portrait of Dr. Botox. If you ask me, the version in oil looks better than the one in the flesh.

At last the men return, Marc to my side, the old playboy to the chair behind his sculptural desk. For long seconds, silence flies over our heads. Then Dr. Fontaine scratches his throat.

"Zoe...It's Zoe, isn't it?"

"Mm," I answer, wanting to show them that I, too, can speak the sophisticated language of doctors.

"You look like an informed young woman," Fontaine says, his voice smooth and sinuous as he patronizes me.

"Cut the crap!" I want to say. But only my eyes say it. I think he understands.

"I recommend a biopsy," he ejaculates.

I turn toward Marc.

"Do I have cancer?"

Marc, who has been sitting silent and straight-backed since his examination of the mammograms with Dr. Fontaine, takes my hand.

"We don't know yet. A biopsy will let us know for sure."

"Isn't that why I had my breasts pressed like pizza crust in the first place? To know for sure?" I want to keep calm, but my breathing is picking up speed.

Marc squeezes my hand and plunges into my gaze. For a moment, all I see in his glance is love as profound as the night. Had this lasted longer than a fraction of a second, I would have remained in shock for the rest of the day. But soon his eyes regain their cloudy, professional composure.

"It's hard to see with the way you're made," he states.

"Lumpy-bumpy," I answer.

"That's it," Fontaine adds.

"Who will perform this biopsy?" I ask.

"A radiologist."

Did Dr. Fontaine just say, "A radiologist"? Did I hear him right?

"A…what?!"

Now the doc assumes his favorite expression: a condescending smile that says, "I am the doctor, handling an impatient patient whose ability to think logically, whose emotional balance, let's face it, cannot match mine." I answer with my special smile (classified in my archives of grins as No. 7b), the one that states, "I want to slap you, you overdyed, over-Botoxed, over-the-hill *fool*!" Of course, he interprets my smile as a manifestation of my admiration of his brilliance.

How I wish I had taken Ziggy II with me, so he could have made a meal of the good doctor's red-soled Louboutin shoes.

"Yes, Ms.…uh…Zimmerman. Zoe. Nowadays, radiologists can do biopsies. At least…uh…a special kind of breast biopsy. The type that will not damage your pretty little…uh —"

Now anger rises up within me, and it rises Everest high. I am about to get up and leave. Marc sees this and takes hold of my arm. I try to escape from his grasp, but he looks at me as if I were a spoiled little brat. For a moment I am frozen. Two seconds later, I am inflamed. The tropics follow the North Pole in no time. Shaking, I remain on my chair, tighten my lips, and let my feet beat the cadence of some imaginary tune.

"The procedure is called stereotactic breast biopsy," Doctor Fontaine goes on in a voice filled with self-satisfaction, and with a smile filled with idiocy that wants to be irony. "It is actually a two-phased procedure. The first phase involves finding the exact location of the lump. We call this imaging."

Marc's hand is still gripping my arm, and it is starting to hurt me. I make all the effort in the world to look at him amorously. He relaxes now, his face beaming gloriously. That's when I kick him on his tibia. Now I am beaming while his face is as contorted as poor writing. I read both surprise and affection in the glance Dr. Fontaine gives Marc. No doubt he attributes his former pupil's expression to anguish, which touches him; yet there is even less doubt that he thinks that, no matter how much Marc may care for me, a doctor should always maintain his cool. Interrupting his prepared discourse on boob biopsy, he sends Marc an indulgent look, followed by, "It's OK."

And then he goes on.

"After imaging, the radiologist takes a sample of the tissue…"

"That is the biopsy," Marc adds in an icy tone, turning toward me with an equally chilly look. He is eager to recover his professional stature in the presence of his mentor.

"Exactly," Dr. Fontaine says, his tone a bit dry. This man does not like his recitations to be interrupted. "During the whole procedure, you will place your breast through an opening in an elevated tabletop. The radiologist will work underneath the tabletop so as to easily access the breast…"

Hey, if you can access codes and accounts, why not access breasts?

"Your breast will be slightly compressed. Many women say that since they're in a prone position…"

Yeah, prone to look like cows.

"The radiologist and his team will take a few x-rays, and you will be asked to hold your breath at certain times. Then your breast will be anesthetized. When this is done, a computer-guided needle will enter your breast and extract some tissue. You will hear a series of clicks as this happens. The whole experience should be painless or nearly painless. Are there any questions?"

"Just one, Doc," I utter.

"Yes, dear..."

"How many times am I allowed to moo?"

5

"Damn it, Marc, you could have explained!"

"You wouldn't have believed me."

"Damn right. I have trouble believing it now."

I hear the click of my boots and the click of his shoes sounding in angry unison on the path. We are in Central Park. The winter sun slaps the scene with a clinical light. I have forgotten my gloves, and my hands are freezing. Marc wouldn't let go of them during the whole consultation, which took place indoors. Now that I need his hands, they're nowhere to be found.

"I want to go to the zoo," I say.

"You...what?"

"The Bronx Zoo. I want to go."

I hear myself and realize I sound like a brat, but I don't give a damn.

"It's kind of far, isn't it?" he says.

"Not by subway it ain't!" I retort.

"But there are no cows at the Bronx Zoo. Are you sure you want to go?"

"Very funny, Marc."

"If I do say so myself—"

I am trembling. Tears start veiling my eyes. I lower my lids so Marc won't see. But I'm too slow. He stops and turns to me, takes my hands, kisses my forehead.

"Darling, you're cold. How about going home? I'll make you a hot cocoa."

"I want to go to the zoo."

We sit on a bench for a minute, and he holds me. "It will be all right," he whispers, his breath a soft breeze across my hair and on my neck.

"You promise?" I ask.

"Let's go to the zoo," he answers, removing his cashmere scarf and wrapping it around my head.

■ ■ ■

Since I arrived in this town, the Bronx Zoo has been an oasis of sorts. I walk up to Seventy-Seventh Street, take the Five Train, exit at East Tremont, and here I am among wild beasts that, unlike the ones in Manhattan, make no compromise. The zoo keeps some of the world's most endangered species, and perhaps I can identify. Last time I was here, I went to the nocturnal exhibit and saw the whole range of wild cats, bats, cloud rats. I told Ziegfried II all about it. "Next time I go, I'll take you," I said, "and you can watch the mole-rat colony in action." Zieg II looked at me, took his little cube of Swiss cheese, and left. His way of telling me, "As if I didn't have better things to do!"

And the time before, there was that middle-aged British lady who insisted on taking my picture. I tried to tell her I hated to pose, and besides, didn't she want to shoot the lions behind me instead? But she only laughed. "But dear, that's the point. I want to take you sitting right here in front of them."

"But why?" I answered.

"Has no one ever told you that you have the hair of a lioness?"

"Yes, but they're wrong."

"Oh?"

"It's the hair of a lion. Lionesses wear their hair short. It's a more practical 'do for hunting. Lions keep theirs free and wild. Why they don't put it in a pony tail is beyond me. With the babysitting and all, don't tell me that cubs don't like to pull on Daddy's hair."

The lady's laughter started in melodic adagios and ended in a symphony for trumpets written by a musically challenged brat. It invaded her body to the point that she almost destabilized herself, despite her sensible shoes. Although I was sure I had never met her in my life, the face was familiar. And then it came to me. She looked just like Agatha Christie.

I have almost forgotten about Laughing Agatha when weeks later I receive a large envelope. How did she get my address? Did I scribble it on a piece of paper and hand it to her? I can't remember. The blank in my memory worries me. Stress does that to you, I hear. It erases pages of your life without warning. Imagine what might happen to the overstressed author. A whole novel could disappear without a trace. Characters lost in the imagination jungle or simply gone on vacation just to annoy the writer. And what kind of FBI cops could solve that one? Hey, what kind?

I open the envelope. In it is a photo of a lion. In front of the lion stands a woman with loose red hair and a rust-colored dress. So she did manage to take my photo. I like myself in this picture. I am in total oblivion there, staring at the lion. There is comfort in my posture.

"There is a peace there. A tranquility," I tell Marc when I show him the photo.

"Yet no docility," he replies.

Funny how men fantasize about female docility yet always run after the wild ones.

There is no return address on the envelope. So I still don't know Laughing Agatha's real name. Nevertheless, I write a little thank you note and send it to Ms. Agatha Christie, Bronx Zoo, Lions' Brigade, New York City. The note is returned to me with "ADDRESSEE UNKNOWN" stamped on the envelope. Much like politicians, postal workers have no imagination.

■ ■ ■

I am lost now, fascinated by the grace of the snow leopards. Three of these Himalayan felines repose before me. Their bodies are freely aligned on a small, rocky hill. I feel tempted to remove my contact lenses. If I did, all I would see would be the sinuous pattern that they are forming, nearly a perfect *S*, white with black flowers freely inked across their supple masses, a luscious serpent caressing charcoal-gray rock; I would see a magical snake instead of the trinity of cats. The leopard on top opens his mouth while looking at the rock, as if about to make some thoughtful observation. The one closer to me just sits, indifferent to visitors, watchful of another space. What space? Perhaps that of another exhibit. I don't know. Maybe a space far, far beyond the confines of the zoo. The cat's glance is elusive, knowing. It's something that the feline owns exclusively; it cannot be shared. The leopard in the middle fixes me with a dreamy, melancholy stare. It's a tender face, and for a gauzy ribbon of an instant, I want to be on the same rock, lying in the same graceful repose. I want to be a leopard, endowed with the freedom of staring long dreamy stares with the ease of animal melancholy.

But soon the beast stretches its elegant body, rises, and walks away. I feel abandoned.

"You're a real cat lover, aren't you, darling?" His baritone comes from behind me. His arms cage my neck and my shoulders; he bends and brushes a kiss on my hair; he whispers, "My little wild one." I turn around. I realize once more how careful a dresser he is. His black jeans mold to his body without being too tight, his white sweater is a mix of black curvy stripes and spots, and his cream-colored overcoat is unbuttoned despite the cold.

I am hungry now and he decides to fetch whatever junk food the zoo has to offer. I see how he stretches his elegant body, how he rises and walks away.

"Let's go home," I say after being satiated. "This place is missing a rat."

6

Marc loves me that night like a young romantic groom from way-back-when enjoying his bride for the first time. We surrender to dreams, our bodies wrapped around each other.

I wake up and extend my hand toward his body. But what I touch is the lacuna sculpted on the pillow by his sleeping form; I feel traces of his warmth, left behind for me to cherish like slowly vanishing souvenirs. With my left hand I reach for my glasses on the bedside table. But I am sleepy, I am clumsy, and I knock them to the floor. I open my eyes. The bedroom looks like a Rothko painting. A huge red spot and not much else. My vision is getting worse. Or perhaps it's only stress. Not long ago, my surroundings without glasses looked like an impressionist tableau. Now they are a flat abstraction.

I take a deep breath, twist my body, extend my arms toward the floor, and finally grab the glasses. I look at the Indian textile covering one of my walls, at its yellow-and-black patterns on a red background; at the wicker sofa I found at a Salvation Army store, to which I applied a vermilion spray and then added a gold cushion; at the bed in disarray, the sheets rumpled like little black clouds, the Mexican blankets packed around me like a scarlet shroud.

There is that ineffable scent in the room, sweet and evanescent. And then his smell. His smell, sea and forest fire, stubborn and blended with the cologne that he even puts on before going to bed. Calvin Klein *Eternity*. Eternity, always. I smile a tight smile and swallow a tear. Damn it, Zoe, why did you let him back into your life again? You know he'll leave just as he's left before. I slap myself, literally, two or three times. Damn it, woman! No more of this.

I talk to myself like this as I get up. As I make myself breakfast. As I wash the dishes. As I shower, as I apply body lotion, as I pick up a fresh towel. As I wipe away tears with the back of my hand.

Outside the bathtub Zieg II is waiting. I realize the poor thing has been following me all morning because he didn't get his cheese. "Sorry, Zieggy boy," I say, "men can be such rats." And you know what? The rodent looks offended. No kidding. "Well, you know what I mean," I finally add while handing him his breakfast. He takes the cheese and looks at me, puzzled. "Yep, it's mozzarella, buddy. I am out of Swiss. It's gonna be one of those days for both of us." The rat looks at me for one additional second to see if it's a joke. When he sees it is not, he starts eating, first slowly and then philosophically. There are worse things to have to eat than mozzarella, after all.

I finish drying myself and throw the towel on the floor, knowing perfectly well Marc won't be there to pick it up. I walk naked to the bedroom closet, and that's when I see them. A dozen bloody spots, in a crystal vase, stand on his side of the bed. The petals are a caress, velvet on stems; the thorns are cat claws. So that's what the vague scent was. Roses. I go toward them with the clear intention of counting the needles, only then I see a white envelope at the foot of the vase. So he left a note. This is new. What do I want to do first, pinch myself with the thorns, or read a doctor's handwriting?

I tear the envelope and see a card printed with Sonia-colored roses and recognize it to be one from the florist on the corner. I open it and, of course, there are Marc's doctor hieroglyphs. What the hell...I spend a whole minute trying to decipher them, and this is what I finally conclude they say:

Darling,
So sorry I had to leave, but the cell phone rang...

So that was the small chime I heard last night. I had thought it belonged to my dream. So he got a new phone. His old one played "La Cucaracha." I am going to miss that. It had charm, not to mention the ability to wake up a regiment of snoring marines.

...and it was Daisy.

Daisy, his wife. His model-gorgeous wife, whom he told he was at a medical convention.

Little Mitch had one of his asthma attacks, and Daisy thinks it's serious. I must go, darling. But I'll be back.

Marc

PS—Hope you like the flowers. Jack Liu (it's Jack Liu, isn't it, the Chinese florist next door?) is such a nice man. He opened his shop at seven for me, and while he was cleaning, I picked these roses for you.

Is this true? Probably. Little Mitch has drawn lines on Marc's forehead for most of the three years of his life. How many times did I pet Marc's hair while he would talk about his son with a trembling voice?

But no more! No more of Marc. No more of his son. No more of his unmentioned yet omnipresent wife. Once he dropped his wallet and the photo of a tall woman with short blond hair slid out. I picked it up before he could react, and I saw within the classical features the sweet expression of those who can afford kindness. Little Mitch, whose picture he had shown me during his times of fatherly anguish, looked exactly like his mother.

"Dammit, Marc! Your wife is beautiful! What do you see in me that you don't see in her?" I get silence as an answer, and a cloud in his glance.

Well, this time he will solve his problems without me. That's it, I am done.

Done.

What do I know about him, really? What do I know about the good Dr. Marc Trenton?

I handle the card for a while, turn it around aimlessly, and then I see it. A small line scrawled in the back: *Don't forget your biopsy tomorrow.*

Now I make confetti of the damn card. I pick up the vase. I want to throw it. Oh, yes, I want to throw it and the damn roses across the room. This will feel good, right? But I stop. Too cliché, I think.

So I put the vase down. As I bend over to smell the roses, a tear falls on a petal.

Damn!

7

Dr. Fontaine has his own clinic, with his own radiologist and his own room equipped for Stereotactic Core Breast Biopsy. "No need to go to the hospital," Marc said. "This is much more comfortable." Much more expensive, too. But why bother making such remarks? The response from a talkative Marc would be, "So what's your point?" The response from a taciturn Marc would be him shrugging his shoulders. But now the bastard is gone. All I have is silence. Silence and fading roses.

I really want to be elsewhere, anywhere. The only thing that brought me here, I tell myself, is my instinct for survival, which is tenacious, and the fact that I'd rather be a cow in a pretty clinic than a cow in a robotized hospital. A nurse who asks me to call her Stella, stout, smiling and middle-aged, leads me with brisk steps to a small room furnished with a white wicker sofa, a white wicker low table looking somewhat related to the sofa, and a small television sitting on a wicker stand (a distant cousin, this one, or possibly the black sheep of the family). Stella opens the stand's two small doors and extracts a disk that she now places in the DVD player next to the TV.

"What are you going to show me, Stella, *Story of O*?"

"Not quite."

"*Emmanuelle*?"

She twists and turns her hand, as if to say again, "Not quite."

I like this woman. I like her mother-earth bearing, the way her face rounds up like a welcoming fruit when she smiles, and the shiny night of her eyes.

"This porno flick should last no longer than fifteen minutes," she says. Cool gal.

The DVD has it all: the gentle masculine voice of the narrator supposed to caress a woman's subconscious and make her feel that she's about to enjoy a stay in the Caribbean; the pastel operating room with a relaxed model lying on her stomach as if she were at the beach; the confident and smiling personnel at the computers underneath, the mothering nurses, and the godlike radiologist. It's the brochure come to life on the screen. So here I am, on my way to paradise.

I have watched a chunk of this masterpiece when Stella returns.

"Well, you have seen enough," she says as she stops the DVD player. "The rest is just babble. It won't bring you more rapture than what you had just now."

"Oh, too bad! Can I see the kinky part again then?"

She smiles a gentle smile and then leads me to the changing room, which is smaller yet than the video room but decorated with the same fake friendliness, and closes the door behind me. *Click*. I remove my sweater and bra and put on one of those lovely cotton robes designed by a tribe of left-handed football players. Where are you, Calvin Klein, when one needs you? I tie the robe on top and see that its left side is two inches longer than the right. So there is style to it after all. Donna Karan and Isaac Mizrahi, watch out! Donatella Versace, mama mia! You've got competition, people!

Stella comes to take me to the operating room. I tell her I am cold. She fetches a blanket and puts it around my shoulders. Looking at this room is like looking at a movie star without makeup. Suddenly, she is not that stunning anymore. Indeed, she appears sadly ordinary. In the video and on the brochure, I saw a spacious room, one that gave an impression of comfort and peace. What I have in front of me is dark and confined. The operating table is less elevated and narrower than expected, and the computers beneath are cramped. Did I say computers? I see just one computer.

I once saw a death chamber on TV. I swear this room looks similar. Only here, the table is elevated, risen above the machinery and equipment so that the operating radiologist can attack my breast from down under. This is insane. This is rape in reverse. Where is the white furniture; where are the cushions with their flowery pastel motif? Where is the odor of lavender spray? Where are the grinning professionals?

And they say Dr. Goebbels was good at propaganda.

When she helps me on the table, I tell Stella what bothers me, and that is not being able to move. I don't know if I can do it—stay immobile with a boob hanging loose from a hole, and wait with utmost tranquility for a hollow needle to pierce it. Imagine a knight piercing another knight with a lance, on a slightly smaller scale. Only I've got no goddamn white horse, no armor, no weapon, except for my mouth. But what can a mouth do against a computer-directed needle on its way to swallow some of your flesh and blood. "Fuck, Stella!" I whisper as the nurse helps me place my breast into the perfectly circular orifice. "There is no way this contraption was invented by a woman!"

"That's what I said," she whispers back. "I wonder what men would say if they had to hang their dick like this!" At this point a man enters the room and begins checking the computer. I can see him from my table. I am above him, feeling as vulnerable as a wounded bird. "This is Dr. Vassick," she says. "Dr. Tommy Vassick. He's a nice guy."

"Perhaps," I say, "but he missed his calling."

"What do you mean?"

"Well, Stella, think about it. The man must be registered as 'Vassick, Tommy.'"

Stella scratches her head and then smiles.

"Oh, I get it. Dr. Vassick Tommy," she calls. "This is Zoe."

The radiologist looks like an aging Peter Pan. Some of his hair has gone on permanent vacation. Round, thick-framed glasses surround his hazel eyes, and his mouth curves up in what looks like a tense half-smile.

Now my boob is hanging from a hole and despite my efforts to imagine myself at the beach in Biarritz, all that comes to mind right now is the word "grotesque." Make that GROTESQUE. Please give me a marquee, and let's illuminate the word. Where the hell is Philip Roth when you need him? If he had gone through what I am going through right now, would his *Breast* have looked the same? I don't think so!

"You don't think what?" Dr. Vassick asks.

"Oh, was I…was I talking aloud?"

"Well, yes. Isn't it the way most people talk? So what is it that you don't think?"

"Do you know Philip Roth?"

"No."

"Ionesco?"

"Heard of. What about him?"

"I wish he were not dead."

"Oh?"

"So he could write some more."

"What about?"

"This."

"This?"

"Yeah. *The Bald Boob of the Soprano.*"

"What?"

I know it ain't Chris Rock or Bill Maher, but I like my joke. I would like to see those guys perform with a boob hanging into space and pretending all is normal and fine. Obviously, the doc doesn't get my 34 C-sized jest. He goes to his computer now and stays silent. Obviously, he thinks I am saying absurd things, like any patient under strain. Maybe I am. Under strain, I mean. As for absurdity, we can compete here. My words against the goddamn, fucking situation.

I feel hands on my back—large and bony eagle's claws attempting to move my body. Not Stella's hands. I lift my head and see a nurse of average size and with a semiskeletal structure. Her face is that of an owl on heroin. If you want to see the eyes of a junkie owl, visit the Fontaine Clinic. Her name is Gertrud.

Until I met Gertrud, I liked birds.

"Now, don't move!" Gertrud's voice has the fractured resonance of a parrot. Eagle, owl, parrot. Damn! I hope the woman will let me subscribe to the Audubon society before making me go through the whole avian index.

"I'll try," I say, adjusting my body.

"Stella will give you a shot to put your breast to sleep. You'll feel a small pinch, and then it should be OK."

OK, my ass. I feel cramped and cranky on this table. I feel like a hostage tied up inside a trunk. I feel like punching the owl with the parrot's voice. I feel the needle inside of me, and the pinch is not such a small pinch. I feel like moving, stretching my right leg a bit, extending my left arm just so, so my body can pretend to relax. I feel separated from my breast, as if it had decided to fly away from the rest of me. Yet I know the hollow needle is in there, deeper now, exploring, picking up flesh and blood on its way. I know my breast doesn't know where it is. I damn well know where I am and I don't like it. I imagine, because it's asleep now, that they could cut into my breast right here, right now, and I wouldn't feel a thing. I feel how hurtful it is not to feel, when what I want is for my breast to go back where it belongs, back into my bra instead of floating above computers to be perforated without its personal consent.

I hear the Gertrud squawk, "Don't move!"

I feel my mouth yelling back, "I am doing my best!"

"Don't move!"

"I'm doing my best!"

And then, Stella's rounded voice: "She already said it was hard for her not to move."

And right after that, the doc: "You're doing OK, you're doing OK."

And now I bury my head and I cry. And I surprise myself. I shouldn't cry, dammit. This is a grotesque situation. A joke to tell friends. A way to sharpen my satirical self. I should laugh. But no, I cry in silence, and then I tense all the muscles of my face and tell the tears to just stop falling. And they do, after some moments of struggle. They do, reluctantly, as if to say, "Hey, Zoe, we need to come out, we need to get some oxygen, we need to let you know that your womanhood has just been violated, and it's OK for us to wander over your face for a while."

Tears are good; tears are intelligent.

I hear: "Oh my God, all this blood, it's all over the place."

It's just a whisper. Apparently, they have hit a vein, and my blood is bursting out like fireworks. I think it might have reached the owl-parrot, and I feel vindicated. "That's what you deserve, you bitch!" I want to tell her. But I restrain myself.

Later, in the recovery room, Stella places a twenty-pound weight on my breast to stop the bleeding.

"It's a first," she tells me when she later comes with a cup of tea. "It took me a while to find something that heavy. Usually, we use a two-pound weight."

So I need a big weight to stop my blood. What else is new?

8

I hardly have enough money to pay for a cab to go home. But I am not allowed to move for twenty-four hours. This means I can't walk to the bus stop, can't go underground to the subway, can't do anything. They have wrapped my boob big-time; I feel partially mummified. Me, I am wrapped up, too—wrapped up in a daze like a Turner tableau without the glow. Everything around me blends. The street scenes, the cars, the skyscrapers, the billboards; all the brouhaha, all the cacophony—it's all the same now. The rain that bites my hands and face seems to be aggressing someone else. Another Zoe, a Zoe detached from me. I am not here. I am a ghost, a mummy; I am the perfect companion for my shrouded breast. Everything is a river, an eclipse where no color is invited. New York is a city of shadows. Damn it, how many painkillers have they given me?

Before the taxi arrives, Stella, who is waiting with me, tells me Marc called. "When he learned there were complications, boy, was he mad!" she adds. I say nothing. Gently she touches my shoulder, as if she knows. Perhaps there is a Marc in her life. I notice she isn't wearing a wedding ring. Sadness shines in her eyes, though not steadily. It comes and goes like the winter sun.

At last the taxi arrives, and Stella helps me out of the wheelchair. The driver is young, handsome, and has trouble speaking English. I finally understand he originally comes from Guadeloupe, but has spent most of his teen years in Paris.

"Oh, *vous parlez français,*" I say, astounding myself. I am in such a drowsy state that I am amazed that my brain is working at all.

"*Oui, madame,*" the young man replies. His voice is cashmere by the fireplace; his voice is cuddling temptation.

"Well, I don't," I reply. "Isn't that a goddamned fucking tragedy?" And I actually kind of mean it. The man seems totally palatable. I bet he's about ten years younger than I am, which makes him more appetizing yet. I'm used to men ten years older, respectable gynecologists in their forties. Come on, Z-Z, I tell myself, you're just out of a relationship. Your bed is not cold yet. So? I don't want a relationship. I just want dessert, another part of me retorts—though perhaps it's the part that has been overmedicated.

"What's your name?" I ask the driver, who does not answer. "*Comment... tu...t'appelles?*"

"Aimé," he says, a broad grin revealing a battalion of sparkling teeth.

"Aimé," I mutter. The name means *beloved.* Beloved, indeed.

"*Et toi, comment tu t'appelles?*" Aimé wants to know.

"Zoe Zimmerman. Z-Z for short."

As soon as he hears this, he bursts into laughter.

"What's so funny?" My French really needs some freshening up, but he finally understands me. Now, he explains something to me, and I really have no idea what he's talking about.

"OK, I try English now." Aimé is animated. He accompanies his broken sentences with broken gestures; he turns toward me, forgets about the wheel. We have a near collision, and car honks around us, sounding something like Beethoven's Ninth played by kindergarteners using toy instruments. We almost die, but Aimé is happy. "It's dick; it's dick!" he keeps repeating with the enthusiasm of someone who has just put a Viagra for brains on the market. That's what "zizi" (pronounced zee-zee) means in French. Imagine that. With a name like this, who needs a lover?

■ ■ ■

Aimé opens the door for me, I pay him and thank him profusely to compensate for the poor tip I give him. Now I am left with a ten-dollar bill in my jeans pocket, enough for milk and a little cheese for Zieg II. I take my key set and open the building door when I feel a hand grab me.

"I take you…là-haut…uh…up. I take you up…up the stairs."

I hesitate.

"Listen, Aimé, you don't need to do that."

I lean against the building wall for a second. Dizziness clings to me like a veil. Maybe I need to wear my glasses. I search through my purse, put them on. But the blur gets worse. I pull the glasses off my face, throw them into my bag.

"OK, Aimé. I believe I need help. Thank you."

Aimé places my arm around his neck and holds my waist.

■ ■ ■

When we reach the apartment, I am out of breath. The door is open. Who is robbing my palace? Aimé looks at me and sees I am as perplexed as he is. We enter. I hear some sort of clatter coming from the bathroom. Four steps and we're there, now the witnesses of a sublime spectacle: the super is bent over the commode, doing his version of a half-moon. The painkiller-induced daze has been replaced by a daze of another kind.

"Il a un vilain cul, ce mec. Il devrait le cacher."

If I understand correctly, Aimé has just declared that the super's ass is ugly, and that he should hide it. I happen to agree. I am also amazed at the way it's all coming back to me. The French, not the super's ass. I realize I know words in French I thought I had never heard.

"Et c'est un vrai con," I add.

Aimé's laugh is clear and exuberant, like a stream on a summer day. He likes my not-so-refined comment. Indeed, the super is a true asshole, and I can say it in French—how about that? For a moment we contemplate, fascinated, the man on his knees, bent over the toilet bowl as if he were praying to it.

"Are you working on the aeration system?" I ask the super.

He twists his liver mouth one way and then the other. I recognize the movement—a type of flamenco for Centrum Silver addicts—as a sign of profound perplexity.

"Mm?" he answers, Jean-Paul-Sartre–like. Between being and nothingness, I can tell where his penchant goes.

"You're venting the system?"

"Whatcha talkin' about? A c'mode got no ventin'."

"I was not talking about the commode," I answer with my gaze fixed on the middle of his back.

He gets my drift and flushes as red as a lobster. Needless to say, his butt remains snow white. He gets up, expresses his indignation by pulling up his pants so high that his package starts to show. It's not so hot in there, either, I think, and suddenly I am getting nostalgic for the view of his ass. He looks at me as if his face were a gun and his eyes, bullets. His upper lip lifts up at one corner, exposing a brownish tooth. If only we could place his ass in his mouth, I think, he would have a better smile, and his brain wouldn't be affected at all.

"A lady ain't suppose' t'look there," he says.

I grab my courage with both hands to confront the threat before me. For the man manages to look more stupid than usual, and this really scares me.

"Why did you change the toilet?" I say. "When I asked you before, you refused to answer."

"Well, the thin' was noisy."

"Didn't I say so many times before? What changed?"

"Well, don't you like it? Got the shape women like these days. Low and modern 'n' all. And here, listen. I flush. Hear somethin'? Hardly any noise at all. Tell ya, the thin's a marvel a' technologistics."

"Technology?"

"Yeah. Ain't that a beautiful thin'?"

"Are you going to tell me what changed your mind or not?"

"Just the damn noise, lady."

"OK. Let me change my question. Are you going to tell me *who* changed your mind?"

He drags his feet toward the door.

"Are you going to ignore my question? Very well. Wait—wait a minute before you leave. Since you're here, I am going to write you a check for the rent. It's not due till the day after tomorrow, but, hey!"

I don't mention that I have exactly twelve dollars and sixty-three cents left in the bank and ten bucks in my pocket, and that if I don't find a job within the next twenty-four hours, I will have to move into a box, possibly under the Brooklyn Bridge, and away from Zieggy II. But I want confirmation of what I already suspect. As I start scribbling, my balance book falls on the floor. (Surprise, surprise! My balance book is out of balance.) Aimé picks it up, holds it for a few seconds and hands it to me.

"No need," the man says when I hand him the check.

"No need?"

"You're in the clear for the next two months."

"And he paid for the commode as well, I bet."

I bet he added a little extra for the trouble, a Ulysses S. Grant or even a Ben Franklin.

"Yeah. Nice guy," he says before closing the door and disappearing.

Nice guy, sure.

Goddamn fucking bastard.

■ ■ ■

I rush to my room and throw myself on the bed. Tears burst from my eyes like stormy waves. Part of me feels buried, drowning, choking; part of me feels immaterial. Part of me is pain; part of me is liberation. Part of me is weighty lead; part of me is a promenade at dusk. Part of me is a breast put to sleep; part of me feels the sun. It is a pale little sun, but strong enough to come through the dusty window and blanket the whole of me. I cry, I cry more, and yet these warm tears feel refreshing somehow. I have found a point somewhere in my own trivial galaxy where pain and pleasure make friends. A point where I simultaneously exist and disappear.

I used to hate Shakespeare. But he was right. To be or not to be, that is the whole damn fucking question.

And I don't want to answer it.

A long shadow has glided through the length of the room. It has lithe limbs, a supple head. It evokes an image of a tree in the desert having a party with the wind. It evokes a vision of a spirit, the silhouette of an angel searching for wings. It has a voice, soothing and warm. A velvet voice.

"Il ne faut pas pleurer."

I follow the pattern the shadow has traced on the floor, on the bed, on part of me, and see that it connects to Aimé. I forgot about him. So he has followed me into the bedroom. He pulls me up, hugs me. "Don't cry. You too pretty to cry—too funny to cry. Z-Z, don't cry. Don't cry, don't cry."

It sounds like a lullaby.

He sits on the bed. I lift my face toward his. He dries my tears with the tips of his long, dark fingers.

"Chérie. Tu es belle," he says, caressing my hair. He does this for a long, long time, putting my breathing on automatic pilot, sending my mind someplace where silence is soothing.

And then his hands brush over my clothes. The sensation is a breeze gently waking my body. I smell him. Pepper and cinnamon. His touch, still gentle, anchors to my flesh now. His hands circle my waist, crawl under my sweater, and undo my bra. His caresses are a river flowing on my back. He presses me against him. I can feel his hardness. He has removed my sweater, is sucking my free breast, his hand gently resting on the bandaged one, as if to protect it. I want to remove myself, say not now, not now. It's as if he has read my thoughts, for he stops. But I want this; I want him.

He looks around the room, gets up. He finds a little cushion shaped like a spade, grabs it. It's one of four cushions my aunt from Quebec made for me. The other three were a diamond, a club, and a heart. The diamond lost its shine; the club got lost; and Zieg II decided to remake the pattern of the heart, so it's full of holes now. All I have left from Aunt Yvette is the spade, "the reversed heart with a little tail," she used to say.

He throws his shirt on the floor, and I see the torso of a bronze statue. Aimé. Beloved. Nature loves this man, has chiseled him with the determination of a Michelangelo. He smiles; he is a dark moon shining down on me. He lies next to me, places the cushion on top of my bandaged breast.

His mouth travels to my center. I escape. I don't want too much, too soon. I slide his jeans down, touch his thighs. His magnificent, powerful thighs. I fondle them, fondle his legs, his mountain-climber calves. I kiss his inner thighs, let my mouth travel up. I find his penis. Long, warm metal. I circle it with my tongue. Every time I move, he takes the cushion and shields my breast with it. I want to tell this gentle, careful lover that I don't feel my breast right now, that I don't care about my breast right now. That all my being is gone, that all that is left of me is my need for pleasure, that a merciful god has pressed the key to delete the rest of me. That I can be retrieved with a rescue disk later. I need no cushioning; I need no spade.

He takes my hand. He wants me up. Before he plasters me against the wall, he makes sure the cushion is in place. Now he's convinced my boob is secure. My legs form a white creeper on the dark of his back. He enters me and I burn. He travels underground and I fly into the brass air of pleasure. I come like a bird song; he comes like a long whisper in a grotto.

■ ■ ■

I wake up. The bed is warm, full of scent. Pepper, cinnamon, roses and sweat. So it was not a dream, a marvelous erotic dream, I think when I feel his right arm under my head, his left hand on my belly creeping down.

■ ■ ■

Few words have been shared during our loving. Aimé will go as he came, his voice as warm in his *bonjour* as in his *au revoir*. He will smile, summer clouds on his teeth, sunbathed onyx in his eyes. A passing god of comfort, with rapture wrapped tight around his body and, for an instant, around mine.

■ ■ ■

I watch him dress while I let the sheets enshroud me. I rub my skin against the remnants of warmth and musk that he has left for me as a gift. Something falls on my face. I touch it. A petal. A rose petal. I brush it away.

"You're a good lover," I tell him, holding my bandaged breast.

He pulls his jeans up, smiles.

"It's not hard," he answers.

He says these few words smoothly, with no audible accent.

"Perhaps not now," I joke.

He buttons his shirt, his head bent down.

"Thank you," I add.

"Pourquoi?" He tucks his shirt in, sits on the bed, reaches for his immaculate Adidas.

"Why? For letting me forget about my life for a sweet moment."

His face tightens.

"What's wrong?" I ask.

I hear silence, his silence, dense like a crypt.

"What's the matter?" I insist.

"Tu penses...you think...this is just...once? How do you Americans put it? Just for one night?"

"A one-night stand, you mean."

"Aimé doesn't do one-night stands," he says.

"You mean you...want to see me again?"

He gets up, turns his back to me.

"I have offended you." I rise, wrap myself in a blanket.

"Oui," he whispers.

"I'm sorry." I take his hand.

"So you wanted me to make love to you just once?"

"That was more than once, Aimé."

He laughs. I touch his face.

"How about once more?"

"You just showered and dressed. Don't you have to go to work?" I tighten the blanket around me.

"Quelle heure est-il?" he asks.

"About ten to eight."

"Once more, then." He takes my hands off the blanket, which falls at my feet. His hands contour my head, my shoulders, my waist, my hips, my legs. He sits on the floor, takes my hand. "Chérie," he whispers, "come to me." I lower myself to a crouching position. He lays down. I crawl on top of him.

I feel something furry under my hand.

"Zieg II, later!" I say.

9

So much for not moving for the next twenty-four hours.

I swallow pain killers and look out the window. Snow. A new day in a wedding dress. I hate wedding dresses but I enjoy the clean view. The soreness that loving has wrapped around me feels paralyzing but delicious. I almost forget about the $12.63 in my account. Aimé, who has just left, wanted to lend me some money. I refused. Not wise, I tell myself. I could have used the fifty dollars he handed me.

"I lend this to you. Not give. You understand? But you need money."

"I don't."

"Twelve dollars in the bank. It's very little money in America."

I realize he must have seen what was left on my account when he picked up the balance book.

"You're *fauchée*."

"Fowchay?" I ask.

"Yeah. Fauchée. Let me think. It means…no money. It means…I know. Broken. You're broken."

"You mean, broke?"

"Voilà! That's it. Broke."

"Broke and broken, actually," I say.

"Then take my fifty." He lifts me, smacks me on the lips.

I kiss his neck. "No."

He said I was beautiful but very têtue. Stubborn. But I can't afford to take money from a man. Not anymore. I light a cigarette, sip my coffee. Aimé made it this morning, and it's as thick as blood. I go to the sink, empty half of my cup, and add hot water from the rusty faucet. Coffee is more digestible to my poor American stomach now. I think I should visit Italy, France, Spain, any country where they make coffee so dense it can walk on its own. The closest I have come to that was when Ziegfried and I were sent to Québec. We went every summer, until Uncle Ray and Aunt Yvette (*Tatie Yvette*, we called her) died in a car accident. Some drunk took a U-turn on the interstate. There were no survivors. Tatie Yvette taught me all the cool expressions in French, the slang, the dirty jokes, the dirty songs. She gave me my first cigarette and my first condom. I miss Uncle Ray. I miss Yvette more. Her petite figure, her nose twitching with amusement, her eyes so large and so brown and so ready to swallow the world in one gulp. Her dancing, so light and so comic in the streets of Le Vieux Québec. Her laughter sounded like chimes in the wind. She would spend April in Paris. "Next time, you'll come with me," she said. And the following year it was all set. We were going to leave the first week of April. She died on April first. April Fools' Day indeed. Suddenly Paris was on another planet.

Some day, I'll go there, live there even, be tough and sophisticated. I'll be an author then, do outrageous things that will shock even Parisians, like Colette. I'll eat chocolates. Drink cup after cup of dark coffee. Dedicate my books to Yvette.

■ ■ ■

Will Aimé come back? Intimacy is a good illusionist. He will see another woman, younger, nearer his own age, with more tender tales and less history. She'll have no worry lines on her face, no visible cracks in her soul, and possibly more than $12.63 in her fucking account.

■ ■ ■

I grab my coat, scarf, and hat, and run down the stairs. The cold stings my cheeks; traffic roars, with an occasional screech. I run ten steps, buy today's *New York Times*.

Back in the apartment, I pour a demitasse of Aimé's coffee. A half demitasse—I add water to it like before. Tomorrow, I'll only add 40 percent. One day, I'll be able to take it full force. But right now, I can't think about coffee. I have to find a job. I open the paper, grab a pencil, and begin my quest.

One page falls on the floor. It has a large picture of the president wearing his usual smug smile, above which the headline reads, PRESIDENT CONFIDENT DEMOCRACY WILL SPREAD IN MIDDLE EAST. I leave the page where it is; it belongs on the floor. I flip to the employment section in the classified ads. Just as I start to scan the ads, I feel something between my feet. Zieg II. What does he want? He already had his cheese. I look down. The rat is right on the president's head, making the type of deposit between his eyes that cannot be made in a bank.

■ ■ ■

I have walked the streets, given resumes to doctors' offices, insurance companies, applying for anything requiring typing and computer skills. I have knocked on the doors of import/export, office supply, and retail stores. I have even applied at schools in need of full- or part-time secretaries. I have even gone into the NBC office and asked, red nosed and cold handed, if Dave Letterman needed a new assistant. After all, I have nothing to lose. I have gone as far as giving nods of approval to all the political grunts made by a prowar prospective employer. I feel like a traitor. I'll seek consolation tomorrow morning when I call Zieg II at paper-reading time.

When I enter the offices of the mighty Chancecastle Publishing Company, my body trembling and my head aching, it is night. I let myself collapse on a chair in the reception area and for a minute, I forget the notion of time and place. I just want warmth and a little respite. I close my eyes and massage my forehead in an attempt to regain my spirits.

"You look like you could use a hot cup of tea," I hear someone say.

The voice is gentle yet rooted. I open my eyes and see before me a pair of sensible shoes. I lift my head and...

"Oh, my! But it's...it's Agatha Christie!"

"I beg your pardon, have we met? Oh, dear! The hair...of course!" she laughs.

"Thanks for the picture," I say, rubbing my arms.

"Oh, you liked it? Good, good! I've been to the zoo since then, and I was hoping I'd see you there again...But tell me, how did you find me?"

"I didn't."

"Oh?"

"I have spent the entire day giving out resumes, filling out applications. I was going back home when I saw a light on in your building. I thought, why not? Plus it was cold and..."

"Well, Zoe...it's Zoe, isn't it? Come into my office."

It takes all I have to find the energy to get up. I follow her like a zombie.

She turns back, smiles at me, and goes to the receptionist, a small young man with limp blond hair and an expression to match. "Danny, bring us some tea, will you? Peppermint, perhaps. Yes, I think peppermint is what we need right now."

"Please sit down, dear." She indicates the cozy corner, two nineteenth-century armchairs and a sofa, upholstered in red and yellow stripes in a vast office filled with antiques. Further and toward the center of the room, the desk, with its brown computer and a tall seat behind, reminds me of a throne. Is Agatha Christie an enlightened monarch? At this point I am grateful I am invited in the less intimidating part of the office.

"By the way," she says, "my name is Terry Chancecastle."

She observes me for a moment, grins, and then adds, "Although, you know, I do sometimes wish it were Agatha Christie."

10

Before I help myself to some breakfast, I give Ziegfried II a piece of Swiss cheese. He eats it with the quaint manners particular to rodents, holding the cube of cheese between his front paws, his mustache twitching as he nibbles. He is one happy rat, and has been for the past two weeks, ever since I got hired by Agatha Christie, aka Terry Chancecastle. I'm happy, too. It's nice being able to afford something besides mozzarella.

I am now an associate editor at Chancecastle Publishing. I correct how-to's, among them some that need serious fixing; self-helpers helping the self-centered take a serious look at their belly buttons; gardening editions having trouble with the root of words; doctors' titles with diseased grammar. I give a facial to these little masterpieces by cleaning up prepositions and tweezing out adverbs. Call me a book beautician. I make volumes ready for readers. People will buy these little boxes of words, these diluted solutions they can easily digest. They will read a page or two, take a deep breath, smile and imagine they have now become the new Dalai Lama or Dr. Phil revisited.

Can't complain, though. Blue Cross/Blue Shield, dental plan, vision plan, it's all in the package. I consider myself lucky. Nora, a twenty-eight-year-old with long brown hair and a mousy face, told me that before she was hired by Chancecastle Publishing, she had been hopping from company to company, each promising her a health plan in the next six months. After having employed her for five months and three weeks, each of the companies reduced her hours from full-time to part-time, making her ineligible for benefits. Clever. I could use the strategy with men. The reduced-hours thing is appealing to me.

These companies hate Terry Chancecastle, I suppose. So does her brother Donald, who is number two in the company and not happy about it. He believes employees should be treated like serfs. His sister thinks that employees are more productive when they are treated with respect. Once hired, they're covered. Of course, she expects hard work in exchange. She's a bit of a taskmaster. But she works harder than anyone else. Cathy, who does her typesetting next to Nora's desk, tells me Terry is often at the office until eleven o'clock at night, and sometimes even till midnight. Though I wonder how Cathy knows this—doesn't she leave at five like the rest of us? Cathy has worked for the company forever. Frankly, I can't use my writer's imagination to envision Cathy as a child, or as a young girl kissing for the first time, or as a woman in the arms of a man. Or another woman. She is as frail as a November branch, has white hair and bright little eyes, and wears dark pantsuits. Miss Marple in Manhattan.

Agatha must be alone, very alone, to drown herself in her work like that. She doesn't get along with Donald, Cathy tells me, and the two have had many arguments late at night when the building is mostly deserted. Cathy seems well informed. Does she work into the wee hours, too, to distract herself from her own loneliness? Also, is she the ever-faithful employee, or does she spy on her boss? My boss, too. My lonely boss who, I suspect, doesn't have anyone waiting for her at home, not even a cat.

Actually, there is a reason for this. If a cat doesn't wait for her, it's because she takes Barnaby to work with her every day. With black hair pointing from his ears like exclamation marks, a clean little white beard under eyes that mean business, Barnaby is one intimidating cat. An aristocratic feline that will accept no crap or its asshole and will have either for lunch if it gets in the way. That's when I decide to rename Barnaby "Lord Barney." Under his champagne, black spotted coat there must be about sixty pounds of muscle. I have seen a couple of bobcats back in PA, but this guy is not from here. Barnaby is a European lynx. I'm not sure pet lynxes are legal in central Manhattan, but rich people can transcend annoyances like, say, the law. These days I look forward to her morning grand entrance with Lord Barney on a leash. Most employees are scared of the cat. I tell them that there are animals more dangerous than lynxes. "Name one. One in the vicinity," they ask. "Look around you," I answer.

"You!" they joke. "You're Dangerous Zoe! Ha, ha, ha!"

"Ha, ha, ha!" I reply. Morons!

■ ■ ■

"Hey, Lord Barney!" I call to the lynx the first time I bring some corrected pages to Miss Chancecastle. "Nice to meet you!" We shake paws. One corner of Agatha's mouth is smiling—the corner she thinks I am not seeing. Lord Barney looks at me funny and then decides I am OK. Follows me around, growls at a few choice editors in the room before he reaches my desk. I see the editors shaking. Most of them are men. Lord Barney gets close to them, and if their bodies were buildings, we would have a revised edition of the great San Francisco earthquake.

Lord Barney is like ex-lax for these scaredy-cats.

11

"You're always served first, aren't you Ziggy?" I tell the rat, watching him as he daintily eats his Swiss cheese. "Now I can get myself some breakfast." I drag my feet from the refrigerator to the microwave, from the microwave to the counter top. I feel like a dervish dancer stuck in a shoe box. Round and round and round; bump and bump and bump. Ouch!

I pour milk into my cup. Some of it gets on my face. So does cocoa powder when I try to mix it with the milk. No dog to lick my cheeks—what a waste. I place the cup in the microwave, and before I can close the door, it swings to close itself and bangs my head. It's Saturday morning; I'm barely awake. But a crispy croissant sits waiting for me on the Formica table, and I manage a smile.

Ding. Ding-ding. "Is that the doorbell at this hour?" I ask Ziggy. I cross the immensity of my palace. It can't be Aimé, can it? He works on Saturdays.

It isn't Aimé. What I see is a young man built like a broom. Dressed like a broom, too. He has on a pair of Drew Carey glasses, only he doesn't have the cheeks or the smirk to carry off the look properly. Pimples sprout like mushrooms on his skinny face.

"What can I do for you?" I ask while shooting a quick glance at my cocoa and croissant. If I don't get rid of Mr. Broom here in thirty seconds, they'll need another visit to the microwave, at which point one will lose its taste and the other its crispiness. Can't a girl be an uninterrupted gourmet?

"Have you seen a rat?" His voice seems derailed, rusty.

"A rat?" I proclaim, trying to block his view—it's my five feet two inches against his gangly six-three frame. But how tall do you need to be, really, to hide a rat?

"Yeah, I have been looking for it for weeks now. Was the best rat, too."

"What does your rat look like?"

"Black and white. A lab rat."

Ziggy, I hope you're in your hole.

"Now, mister...what's your name?"

"Ernest Herald Clifford Guillermo Gonzalez-Bhattacharya, the third!"

"Yeah, yeah. Right. Look, Ernest—"

"It's a matter of great importance," he says hurriedly.

"Why would it be of great importance being Ernest?" I smirk.

"What? No, the rat. The rat is of great importance."

OK, I am perfectly aware that I wouldn't get a medal for my Saturday-morning wit. But I am trying to gain some time here. I turn around. No Ziggy. Good boy.

"So you lost a rat, Ernest?"

I frown, rub my eyes.

During a moment of inattention, the broom-man gets in without an invitation. I don't know what to do. I still have some leftover rural PA sense of hospitality. Doors are still kept open over there, and neighbors come and drop cakes and the latest gossip at any time of the day. But a little of NYC is setting in as well.

I indicate a corner on the sofa where it's no longer plush. Springs dance the fandango there, and they will surely hurt his skinny butt. That way, he can go quickly, and let me and his rat have our breakfast. He makes a face when he sits down.

"So what's the name of your pet?"

"It is not a pet. It doesn't have a name."

"What do you do with a rat then?"

"I conduct experiments."

"For what?"

"Cosmetics companies."

"So you're the employee of a cosmetics company. Which one?"

I hope he won't name any of the companies that manufacture my shampoo or makeup, for I make sure the products I buy clearly state, "This product has not been tested on animals."

"I'm freelance."

A freelance animal tormentor, ain't that nice. The doorbell rings again.

"Excuse me," I tell Ernie III—the Emperor of Torture.

I open the door. A mass of red hair bends to kiss my cheeks and then slides a finger down one of them and licks from its finger part of my breakfast that landed on my face earlier. Ziegfried—the original Ziegfried—attempts to send his finger on another ski trip down my cheek, but I stop the slalom and slap his hand away.

"How did you get in the building?" I ask him.

"How about, 'Hello, my dear brother, how nice to see you'?"

"Ziegfried, my beloved brother! How nice to see you! Now, how did you get in? This is supposed to be a high-security building!"

Do I sound convinced?

"High security, my ass! An old lady from the second floor, Mrs. Tatandos or something like that…"

"Mrs. Papandopoulos," I correct.

"Yeah! Well, she arrived at the building the same time I did. She asked me to hold her grocery bag while she opened the door with her key. She said, 'You look like a nice man,' and let me in just like that. I carried her stuff to her apartment. Jesus! Have you seen her place? It's full of birds: doves, parrots, love birds, budgies, everything with wings."

Great! If the next Jack the Ripper turns out to be cute, Mrs. Papandopoulos will invite him in to sing with her canaries.

"You look a mess, sis."

It's not something I want to hear on an empty stomach.

"Ziegfried!" I start yelling. "I—"

"Oh my God, it's my rat!" Ernest exclaims.

Oh no! Ziggy II got out! He thought I was calling him! Now the pubescent sadist is trying to catch him. Ziggy is in a frenzy. He goes right, turns left, follows an oblique path, and beelines it underneath the sofa; and then he comes out again. If his course could trace a pattern, it would be an impossible maze. And he does it at full speed, in a panic. I run after Ernest, bang my head against the wall. Ziegfried (the rat) doesn't move. Ernest gets close to him, but before he can make the capture Ziegfried (my brother) wraps him in a bear hug. Ernest freezes like—well, kind of like a stunned rat would.

"I got him," Ziegfried says. "What do you want me to do with him?"

"Give him to me," I reply.

"OK."

My brother maneuvers the captive over to me. Ernest's glasses go flying in the process. I see that his right eye says hello to his nose while his left one wants to say good-bye to his face. I grab him by the shirt with both hands, stand on my tiptoes, and yell up at him, "Listen, you rodent-bully! Who do you think is the pest here? If I catch you touching so much as an ant, I'll send you to the *Lord of the Flies* before you can scream Retin-A, you spotty bastard!"

I push him out of the apartment, pick up his glasses and throw them at him. Now I slam the door behind him, and when I turn I see Ziegfried and Ziggy II looking at me with roughly the same expression of open-mouthed astonishment. Ziggy II seems out of breath. I go to the kitchen and get him a piece of cheese. I hold it out to him, and he takes it greedily and runs to his hole. Clearly, it will take me a while to regain his trust. It might be days before he shares his meals with me again.

Speaking of meals, I contemplate my now-cold chocolate milk and croissant with a touch of nostalgia.

12

"What did I just do?" Ziegfried says.

"How come you have a suitcase with you?" I ask.

"Did I just help you attack a man I have never met before?"

I smile at my brother.

"Did you?"

He looks at me, somewhat stunned. The rings under his eyes look like question marks.

"I'm hungry," I add.

My brother's chin goes up and down several times before he says, "Me too."

He still sounds like a trombone. If only he could sing, I wouldn't mind hearing some blues right now.

"So what's with the suitcase?" I ask again.

"Let's eat first," Ziegfried says while opening the kitchen cabinets. "There's nothing here."

"There is a chocolatine in the fridge," I declare.

"Aren't we a fancy girl now? French pastries and all."

"Yeah," I retort. "Goes with the luxury of the place, don't you think?"

He looks around but makes no comment.

We sit at the artfully scratched, bowlegged Formica table. "There's chocolate in the middle of this," Zieg says, examining the pastry.

Duh! I think. Why else would the thing be called a *chocolatine?* I feel tempted to ask my brother if his gray matter has gone on vacation to the Caribbean. Instead, I say, "Well, do you want to swap? There is no chocolate in my croissant."

Did I mention that, since the visit of Ernest III, the croissant has been microwaved twice? If you put a croissant in the microwave long enough, it can do yoga positions on its own.

"Do you mind?" he asks.

"You're my guest, Zieg, and I haven't seen you for such a long time. Help yourself!" I hand him my croissant with the expression of the ultimate Pieta. He looks so grateful.

I dip my crisp chocolatine in my café au lait with delight. He lifts his croissant to his mouth. Like I said, with the microwave's assistance, the croissant has become an expert in Hatha Yoga. Zieg is cross-eyed for a moment. I can tell he's wondering if French pastries are supposed to do the Camel Pose with such ease.

"How do you like the croissant?" I smile my loveliest hypocrite's smile.

"Is it supposed to be so...elastic?"

"Oh, absolutely! That's what makes a croissant so special. You can extend it, twist it around your finger—all that good stuff. Trust the French for making sweets able to do their own gymnastique!"

He gives me a look that says, "City air is doing funny things to my sister."

After we're done eating, I serve him black coffee; he takes a sip. "Jesus! This is strong! Since when do you make coffee like that?"

I take his cup, empty it halfway, add some water, and put it before him on the table.

"There," I say. "Now tell me what you're doing here."

"You know. He called."

"Who?"

I know damn well who.

"Marc. He said you've been avoiding his calls for the past two or three weeks."

"Did he also say that he's still married? Zieg, I'm tired of being the other woman. Fucking on the sly is not my kind of thing."

"His boy almost died, did you know that?"

I swallow saliva. So he's going to stay married, guaranteed. For the kid. I can't blame him for that. But I can't go on like this.

I just can't!

"He has this absolutely gorgeous wife. Far more beautiful than I am. And—"

"Jesus. You don't know." My brother's deep voice is muted; I can hardly hear him.

"Don't know what?"

"About Marc's wife. Everyone in Noliar knows. How come you don't?"

"I don't live there anymore, remember?"

"But everybody knew, even when you lived there! Jesus, girl!"

For a moment, silence wraps us like a shroud. Then Zieg clears his throat.

"Marc's wife is a di—a lesbian."

This time, the silence hits me with a hammer.

"I can't believe he never told you," Zieg mutters as if speaking to himself.

Well, I can believe it. How offensive it must be to a man like Marc not to be desired by his own wife, to have rivals who are women. For testosterone torment, you could hardly do better. The news does not console me, however. I see how he sees me now: the convenient mistress. Better yet, the other wife, the one he can make love to. The one who can restore his afflicted ego. The small woman that he can dominate with his height and his medical degree.

"I don't want to talk about it anymore."

"But, Zoe—"

"You know, Zieg, you still haven't explained the suitcase."

"Jesus, Zoe, can't a guy visit his sister for a few days?"

"You hate big cities. Tell me what's going on."

Silence sets in, stretches, breathes.

"I resigned," he finally mutters.

"I thought your job at CompCommute paid well."

"You don't understand. I resigned from everything. My job, my life!"

How many shocks can a woman endure on a Saturday morning?

"No! You left Vivian?"

I never liked my sister-in-law. A pretty, tight-packed woman who half destroys her looks with her absolute lack of charm. Her bitter mouth and the way she uses it with that dry, staccato tone of voice. How someone can be like that and not get major osteoporosis is a mystery to me. But Vivian the Bitch is in top form. She hates Hollywood, vegetarians, and universal healthcare. But the truth is, she was devoted to Zieg. So I as long as I had Advil in my purse, I tolerated her right-wing insanity.

"Yes," he mumbles.

"Just like that?" An idea comes to my mind. "Did you tell her you were leaving her?"

"I said I was going away. Isn't that enough?"

No, I want to tell him. Not with Vivian. But what do I know? Had Zieg told her he was leaving her for good, she might have rented a machine gun and made hamburgers out of him.

"The sofa is yours; sleep on it at your own risk," I warn him. "Springs are trying to get out and will attack you when you least expect it."

"I won't stay long, anyway," he declares.

"You can stay until you find a job. We'll manage."

"Jesus, Zoe, you don't get it, do you! When I said I resigned, I meant from everything. My job, my marriage, this life, this country."

"This country! Where are you going?"

He looks tense and his face is as red as his hair.

"Jesus! Do I have to spell it out for you?"

"As a matter of fact, yes."

"I am going to Tibet, to become a Buddhist monk."

Wow! Did I hear that right? I wonder about my brother's sense of transition. I mean, how do you go from computer specialist to monk, from a mouse to prayers?

"You realize that, for a Buddhist monk—a formerly half-Jewish Buddhist monk—you say 'Jesus' a lot. Perhaps you should alter your vocabulary a bit before you go."

"Perhaps you should alter your smartass attitude, especially now, when both our worlds are collapsing."

He's right. There is an earthquake inside of me; I shake all over. He comes to me, hugs me. It feels smooth and comfortable, like a feather mattress. I finally free myself from his hold. I need to regain my composure, act like a sister again. I have a good strategy for that. Criticize his appearance. It's mean, but it works. A sister's got to do what a sister's got to do. What's family for, anyway?

"You've gained some weight there, Zieg. Should I write the Dalai Lama and tell him to plan a special diet for you?"

He sends me the placid look of the crocodile annoyed by a bug, but not annoyed enough to interrupt his nap to kill it.

"When are you leaving?" I add.

"In a week or so. I wanted to spend time with you before that."

I look at him. There is something else. Something else behind his visit that he's not telling me. Sure, he left his computer specialist position for the lotus position, and panting in bed with his lithe little wife for prânâyâmâ breathing with a gaggle of Tibetan men wearing red-and-orange robes. An excellent exchange, I'd say. But my sister sense is telling me that there is definitely something else he's leaving out.

I am simultaneously in shock and overjoyed. I want to applaud Zieg for leaving his fascist wife. The shock comes from my brother's plan to move to Tibet, a country where half of the population fled from Chinese oppression. I don't know much about Tibet, other than that one out of five of its men is a Buddhist monk; that a rising superpower attempted to crush its culture and partially succeeded; and that a Hollywood superstar, while desperately trying to get the world to pay attention to the abuse, is still blowing in the wind. So I wonder, will my big brother become a meditating monk there, or part of the Tibetan resistance, or both?

Or does he just want to meet Richard Gere?

With the exception of Gere, all of this is unsettling. It's a good thing I have my butt on a chair, otherwise I would become the Leaning Tower of Pisa, only five foot two and with freckles. I grab the *New York Times* to regain my composure. I glance over the main titles, see that our president has brought a new world disorder and that his minions are rushing to congratulate him.

Dammit! The whole world is becoming a Tower of Pisa. And it's leaning to the wrong side.

I go to the entertainment section. "So you're staying a week, eh? Well, what do you want to see?" I run my index finger across the art show section to see if there is some kind of Tibetan art retrospective, so Zieg and I can somehow get a glimpse at his future, but my finger suddenly stops and I exclaim, "Well, I'll be!"

"You'll be what? Nuts? I think you're beyond that, Zoe."

OK, so Zieg scored a goal. I don't like it.

"Marcel Pavie is having a retrospective!" I finally say after sending my brother a few choice glances. "At the MoMA, no less."

"Morsel Payview? Isn't that the guy who was arrested for murder in Noliar a few years ago?"

"Three murders. The pastor's wife and their two kids," I reply.

Zieg looks absent now. His eyes travel through the kitchen window. My own decide to take the ride, too. Seen through the window, the city takes the appearance of an old postcard, its colors withered by the dust on the glass, its skyscrapers humbled by the haziness. I have been meaning to Windex the damn window for the past few weeks, but now, I don't know if I will. I kind of like this transcendental New York, the city flattened yet more palpable, like something you can hold in the hand, a soothing souvenir. I am not sure what Zieg is thinking. He's somewhere else.

Finally he asks, "Do you think he did it?"

"What?"

"Morsel, I mean, Mysoul. Do you think Mysoul did it?"

I roll the newspaper into a tight cylinder and whack my brother on the head with it. Maybe his little gray cells will flicker back to life and straighten up.

"No. Because he didn't do it. Don't you remember who did?"

Apparently not. I wonder if the Fontaine clinic can do some stereotactic procedure for the memory of redheaded computer men soon to sport red habits. How can Zieg not remember what happened? The man who did it used to give me the creeps, even before the murders, and despite his position in the community.

Zieg massages his head.

"So why did they arrest Mysoul? Damn, my mind is a blur."

I guess I failed to straighten out his gray matter. Maybe I should hit him again. He's a computer specialist, after all. He's been at it so long, he probably functions like his own freaking machines. Click on a program icon twice and go where you want to go.

"It's all that fucking shit—" he adds in a whisper.

"Well, if that doesn't sound like a true yogi, I don't know what does." I take a deep breath. "Mar-cel," I articulate, "not Mysoul or Morsel. Though God knows he's appetizing…Too bad I'll never be able to have a taste of him," I add.

"You really think he's that good looking?"

"Is that a serious question? He looks like Lord Byron, for Christ's sake. And without the club foot. What else do you want?" I smile at the memory of this gorgeous yet unattainable man. "That's his nickname, actually. Byron, I mean. You remember that?"

Zieg looks perplexed for a moment.

"Oh, I get it."

Sometimes I wonder.

"Get what?" I just have to ask.

"Why you can't have Morsel. It's because he's gay."

"Well, aren't we a genius all of a sudden. Everybody in Noliar knew he was gay, you double twit. That's partly why he got arrested."

"Come on, Zoe. Even in Noliar gays are tolerated."

Tolerated—*le mot juste*, as Marcel's favorite writer would put it.

"OK, he got arrested because he's an artist, a free thinker," I declare.

"I suppose that's possible. Though maybe, just maybe, he was arrested because there was evidence suggesting that he was the murderer."

"This culture does not embrace difference."

"Put that shit in your books, Zoe. Or leave it to Jean-Paul Fartre."

"Ha, ha! Very funny! You don't believe me?" I scratch my head. "OK. Pavie also got arrested because he is French."

Zieg shrugs his shoulders.

"He made friends with Unali, remember? What a weird girl! A Cherokee, isn't she?"

"What does that have to do with anything?"

"I don't know, I just—"

Zieg watches as I pick up the paper again and make a new, tighter cylinder with it. I really want to doctor this one, so it will be efficient. Zieg sees what's coming and makes a fence with his hands to protect what's left of his brain. My hit could help him, but for some obscure reason he won't accept my therapy.

Since he won't let me apply my homemade club where it needs to be applied, I tap my hand with it and walk around the room like a headmaster.

"Thank God he had Unali! You know what they did to him in prison? You know what they do to gays in prison? Unali told me all about it. When they let him out, he was a mess. What the hell is the matter with you?" I close in on Zieg. "Put your hands down, so that I can give your head a good whack. It will straighten out your brain, I swear! Come on!"

Zieg looks panicked. Suddenly he sees an old umbrella lying under the table. He grabs it and opens it in no time, and hides under it. It's not a fence; it's a damn barricade. Come to think of it, it's Mary Poppins with fifty pounds to lose.

"Let's drop the subject," the umbrella-headed creature says.

I ignore him.

"We should go see his show. He's one of the greats. Some critics say he's one of the ten best living artists."

"No thanks."

"Why not? It'll be good for your brain and—"

"I don't give a shit about your fucking art, your fucking artist friends, and the rest of you crazy people!" he explodes.

"My fucking art? My fucking art? It took everything—everything fucking thing—everything! You hear me, asshole? It took every goddamn fucking thing for me to move here for my fucking art! It's all I know, you hear me? It's me, me! What I do is who I am, same shit! But you wouldn't know that, would you? You and your fucking...your—"

Everything on him is red. His hair, his face. "My fucking what?" he yells. "Say it!"

"Your fucking cells in your...in your cold heartless compu-tarts!"

"Say what!"

"You think they are better than a good sentence, than a brush stroke? Really? You think they are better than a single heartbeat—even a heartbeat coming out of my shitty artist friends?"

"Who said anything about shitty friends?" Now he's really looking like a lobster.

"You!"

"I thought we were talking about cold cells!"

"You're the one with cold cells!"

"You mean I *was* the one with cold cells."

"Yeah, that wife of yours."

I know he wants to laugh, but he just snickers. He's still angry. "God dammit, Zoe. These stupid cold cells—"

"Let's stop talking about your wife."

"Stop the shit!"

"Okay, enough about fucking cells, wives and computers." I cross my arms and look at him with a tight smile.

"No! It's always your way out, isn't it?" He looks at me like an older brother about to reprimand his rebellious, immature sister. *Male domination slides its way through from century to century. But then again, shit is slippery.* He can go to hell.

"What is my way out?"

"Cracking some silly joke. When you want out of a sticky situation, you crack a fucking joke. Not this time!"

"Are you fucking serious? It's just some silly computer we're talking about!" I frown, then add, "Isn't it?"

Isn't it?

"Oh, sure, who gives a shit about silly computers! Compu-farts, as you put it…"

"Computarts!" I correct him.

"These fucking cells, I have you know, they're not only good for u-tubing Beyoncé. These stupid cells help you keep your…mm… *little masterpieces* protected and secure."

I can tell he's happy with this special injection of sarcasm.

"Pff. You piece of fart!" I give him the finger.

He's smiling now. "And just to add one freaking insignificant detail: these stupid shitty cells can help save lives as well."

"Fuck you, Zieg!"

"Fuck you, Zoe!"

After repeating a couple of more polite "fuck you," a few tears fall.

And then we laugh, we hug, and I say: "Better clean up that language before you leave if you don't want Nirvana to send you a rejection slip."

After a moment, I add, "Are you sure you're ready for this? No more screwing, no more clicking on cute keyboards. It's quite a change."

"Well, you did it."

"I still click on my keyboard and I still screw."

He wraps himself in silence for a moment, then stares at me. "So there is another man."

I walk to the window. From here, the cars below look like Matisse paint strokes—smooth and light. The weekend traffic is less compact, and there is a restfulness in its fluidity. It's a steady stream gliding by. A silent agreement has sailed through hands on wheels, it seems, and drivers maintain a rhythm of clean, quiet waves. The pale winter sun glances in approval at the activity down below. I turn to my brother, who is still sitting at the table. The umbrella is gone. He's playing with a small bit of croissant, stretching it, wrapping it around his ring finger. That's when I notice that he's not wearing his wedding-band.

"Is there anything you would like to see before you leave for Tibet? I realize museums are out of the question." I smile at him. He smiles back; he looks innocent, and he is unarmed. *Now, Zoe, go!* I tell myself. My right hand is tight around my weapon. And so I hit him on his head. I did it, I did it! They claim that since the abolition of outhouses people don't pay attention to newspapers anymore. Who says that kind of shit? I love my *New York Times*.

"Actually, there is," he says, still playing with his croissant.

He sounds normal. My theory has just been validated. So here's the recipe: When a computer man is out of it, thwack his head twice with a newspaper.

"Well, shoot!" I reply. "What do you want to see?" But I realize what he's asking. After a moment of charged silence, I add, "No! Not that!"

"It will be healing," he says.

"Ground Zero is an open wound. Nothing healing about that."

His voice sounds distant.

"I have been there. Once. I don't want to go back. It's still our Hiroshima."

Chancecastle Publishing is three blocks away from Ground Zero. I always take a detour to avoid the view.

"I think it would be healing," Ziegfried repeats.

"Destruction—you find that healing?"

"Seeing death as a new beginning. Your new beginning, my new beginning. Facing the crumbles and the shards of the world and connecting with them. Seeing all the construction, all the projects. It means that things can be built over all this."

"Built over? You mean, hidden, don't you?"

"Please, Zoe!"

"Don't you have enough shards and crumbles in the news? All this dying in wars made for freaking control of the universe, and declared by men who will be far enough away to avoid getting blood spots on their five-thousand-dollar suits, men who think lives—except their own, of course—are little dots on a computer game; men who raise the flag as if it were their own damn fucking erection! Well, they won't get a blow job from me! I am sorry, Zieg, but I don't find death uplifting!"

"Death is not what we think, what the Western world thinks. Death is a renaissance."

"So if we kill people, we're actually doing them a favor?"

Zieg does not reply. He just gives me a tired smile. And suddenly I realize how conditioned we all are by *surface*, by the cover of a book. Here is this six-foot-six man with a pleasant plumpness and thick red hair; a man with big arms to console and a grin to appease; here is this tower of steadiness facing his personal Waterloo, and a future he hopes won't be Saint Helena. He's on to the conquest of spirit now, that of his own, and in his mind his self-imposed exile in a distant monastery is the key to opening up greater spaces, dialogues with the infinite. But still, he's a Western man, a man for whom, for many years now, technology and electronics have been practically a religion; a man whose claustrophobic horizons were set by tiny virtual windows, windows not with views of life but of numbers and codes. Still, what new doors will he be able to open in Tibet? Sure, his existence was rather dull, but it had plush carpets, shiny floors, and a bossy but truly loving wife. He is about to disown all of that. He is about to remove all the gestures he has practiced for the past forty years, click the delete button, and start over. The world he is leaving will soon become a collage of relics, stumbling silhouettes pasted on dead walls.

■ ■ ■

Zieg II is at my feet, his mustache twitching as he looks up at me.

"What do you want? I gave you some cheese just an hour ago."

Zieg throws a piece of croissant to the rat. Zieg II approaches the food, smells it, and turns his long snaky tail to it. I smile, hand him a crumb of my chocolatine. The rat takes it and rushes to his hiding place.

Zieg II understands. He just wants to eat in peace and, mostly, be as far as possible from the overstretched croissant.

13

Ground Zero. A mirror of our fragility. My brother's hand lays wide and warm on my shoulder. I don't see the construction. All I have are the eyes of memory, and they see only the impossible fragments. I look up at the white sky. So does Zieg. I feel caged within the end of the world. Does he feel that way as well?

A glow rises, opening the metallic space. Zieg sees it, too, and the smile he gives me this time is serene. The rays that seem to emerge from the center of the earth are, strangely enough, releasing an absence. The absence of doubt, perhaps. I am not religious, but I love cathedrals. These flat ruins, these graves hidden under new construction, feel at this moment, under this light, like a cathedral. Cathedrals, too, bury their dead. Cathedrals, too, are graves. Isn't Burgos Cathedral the burial place of El Cid?

A big brotherly arm encircles my body like the nave encircles the altar. "Let's go," he says.

My body curves toward the ground, connects to the burnt stone and uncollected flesh. Ziegfried's hand now arches over my shoulder, tightens my structure; and so my back and my head rise up, up, until the whole of me stands straight like a column.

"Let's go now," he repeats.

■ ■ ■

And then it's New York traffic. The speed, the horns, the ebullition. Motors roar, and then they stop, and then they roar again. Same staccato song, same refrain. Rushes and stops, rushes and stops, on and on. Repetition.

Erasures.

We are about to enter Central Park when we hear a honk. The honk is strident, rhythmical, impatient. It's the city. Zieg turns his head to look.

"Just ignore it," I tell him.

"It's a cab driver. Maybe he thinks we want a taxi."

I turn around. Aimé.

His brakes squeak; his smile sparkles.

"Hello, chérie!" he shouts.

Now it's a cacophony of honks and drivers yelling: "Move on, man! This ain't Carnegie Hall!"

"Aimé! You can't stop here!"

Aimé laughs while observing Ziegfried.

"He looks like you. You're just the tea-cup version of him!" He extends his hand out his window to my brother. "Bonjour, I am Aimé. You're Siegfried, yes?"

"Ziegfried, actually. Our parents have issues with the letter *S*. Or a thing for the letter Z. Take your pick."

"You're funny! Your sister never told me you were funny."

"She didn't know."

The irate drivers trace a shaky serpentine path around Aimé's cab, avoiding collisions by some inexplicable urban miracle.

"Aimé! They're giving you the finger! You should go now!" I say.

Unshaken, Aimé responds to the gesture by placing his left fist on his right elbow as his forearm rises.

"This is better than the finger. This is a bras d'honneur."

An arm of honor. You've got to love the sarcasm. Nevertheless, I give Aimé a dirty look.

"OK, I go now. See you tonight."

"Sure," I say. Then I bend to the cab window and whisper in his ear, "No sex tonight. No sex for a week."

His Colgate grin dissolves. He looks at Ziegfried and then understands. "Oh, chérie, he's here for a week? It will be hard for Aimé. No sex for seven long days." He kisses my cheek. He waves good-bye to Ziegfried and yells an enthusiastic "Au revoir!" before rushing back into traffic, nearly bumping into a white Corvette and almost being rear-ended by a bus.

Zieg and I walk in silence, until we find a little cafeteria in Central Park. I order hot cocoa for me, tea for Zieg.

"Your new boyfriend is very young," Ziegfried observes as he helps me carry the beverages to a free table.

I let myself fall into a chair.

"How do you know he's my boyfriend? He could just be a friend."

"'No sex for seven long days!'" he quotes as he grabs his tea.

"So Aimé is not good at whispering, eh?"

"Neither are you. I heard everything." Zieg holds his tea bag like a puppeteer before removing it from his cup. "Listen, this thing won't last."

"What are you, a monk-to-be or a tarot reader?"

He sips some tea.

"He's one of your rebounds."

"You say that as if I collected them."

"You can't stay alone after a serious relationship. You like to lose yourself in another man. Don't you think that's a pattern you should break?"

And all this time, I thought he was immersed in his computers, his wife, and his routine; that my visits were just a distraction, an opportunity for him to subtly patronize someone as he could never patronize his wife. Who would have thought that he actually paid attention to my life? I'm supposed to be the observant one here. I am the writer in the family, for Christ's sake. I sip my hot cocoa, let the whipped cream trace a cloud around my mouth. There is pique in my tone when I finally ask him, "What makes you such an expert on your sister?"

"The love of a big brother," he laughs.

Oh, that! I reflect, Zen-like.

"A big brother who is well aware that his little sister is afraid of love," he adds.

I swallow some cocoa and then wipe the whipped cream off my face with a napkin.

"I am not afraid of love. Look at all the men I have loved!"

"And thrown away," he retorts. "And this young kid…"

"Aimé is very sweet."

"Certainly. And very handsome. And very young."

"So he's young. What do you have against young men?"

"Me? Personally? Absolutely nothing."

"It's not because he's black, is it? Surely you're not a bigot!"

"I am going to ignore what you just said, on the account that you are emotional right now."

"PMS," I mutter.

Zieg laughs.

"PMS, my foot! You have PMS thirty days a month then, even in February!"

"Well! I'll be—"

He ignores my indignation.

"I actually feel sorry for Aimé. You will dump him as soon as you feel he loves you too much. That's what you did with Marc. It's not because he was married or had a son that you left him. It's because you know the man is actually crazy about you."

I take another sip of cocoa, and the whipped cream strikes again. I have now a white mustache.

"I don't think you understand."

A lock of red hair falls in front of his eye. I extend my arm, brush it away—an excuse for me to rummage in my brother's thick mane.

"Let's talk about something else," I say. "Let's go to the zoo."

He takes my hand.

"One more thing, and then I'll stop."

I sigh.

"Just one!"

"You had a biopsy not long ago. How did it go?"

"Just one, but not that one! Pick something else!"

"Zoe!"

"So he told you about my medical history, too? It's a professional breach. He could be...he could be disbarred!"

"Lawyers are disbarred, not doctors!"

Brothers and semantics, that's all I will say.

"Do you know," my brother continues, "the results of your biopsy?"

I decide to give my mouth a rest.

"Do you?" he insists.

Silence rules, doesn't it? And I look good with my mouth closed. Even with a whipped-cream mustache on top.

"You didn't call the clinic, did you?" Zieg continues. "That's what Marc was afraid of. 'She won't call,' he said. For a courageous girl, you can be a goddamn fucking ostrich sometimes!"

"I've got cancer, haven't I?" My voice shivers; my fingernails rake my brother's palm.

My brother takes a deep breath.

"I do, don't I? Well, answer me, damn it!"

Zieg removes my claws from his hand, takes a napkin, and gently wipes off my mustache.

"It's still at a fairly early stage. With chemo and..."

Cars growl and honk. People slide by. Children shriek in the grass and hide behind trees. Worried mothers call out their names. Someone sitting on a bench bites into a crisp apple. Birds collect remnants of an apple on the ground and ask the apple eater for more. Overactive teenagers play punchball. Police cars and ambulances sirens whine. A helicopter purrs over our heads. It's all there. But suddenly I hear nothing. Nothing. All the agitation around me is a silent black-and-white movie. I am the actress who has stepped out of the screen. I am in a cubicle of silence.

And then I break the invisible walls of my cubicle.

I get up and run.

I run in all directions, looking for air, looking for space. Yet New York is a cage. I am the wounded beast. Hell, I am Zieg II racing through his own little imaginary maze and trying to outsmart his pimpled tormentor.

People around us are too blasé to notice me, a woman performing a post-modern version of the Dervish spinners. Zieg finally grabs me.

"Easy, tiger," he says.

"What am I going to do?"

Zieg hugs me. It feels good to be locked into the arms of a man just for comfort.

For comfort. For comfort alone. Not for fucking of any kind.

14

I call the Fontaine clinic. Dr. Fontaine gets on the line. Imagine that. No intermediary nurse, no one but his Botoxed majesty himself, who explains the procedure. I listen, say OK, thank you, yes, of course, thank you, and then I hang up.

I don't want to talk about it. Chemo may work, but he may have to cut off my boob. I repeat, I don't want to talk about it. No, no, no! I go to the shower, scrub myself with soap until I am as red as a Leninist.

After an eternity, I am out of the shower. I must get dressed fast, otherwise I'll be late for work. But my glance stops before the mirror. I notice it reflects back at me the face of bad days. The light of bad days. It's going to trash my reflection big-time. My thighs. Aimé thinks they're pretty. Marc did too, but he always made love without his glasses, so that doesn't count. Plus, face it, what man doesn't like a woman's thighs when he's in the middle of the act? But the mirror ain't in love, and it's showing me cellulite. I think of the feminists who claim that God is a woman.

There is no way a Goddess of mine would invent that jiggly shit.

I must put on that Denise Austin tape. But am I up to seeing big blue eyes popping out of their sockets, and a smile looking like a cut made by a surgeon on hallucinogens? I know what Denise will say, too, at some point, just when every muscle of my body is begging for mercy: *"Let me see that smiling face!"* And to the grinning torturer, I will raise my middle finger;

miraculously, its muscles never tire. The routine never fails. The Marquis de Sade's devotee will play her stretching tricks, and I will respond with the most fit, most supple part of my hand.

But Denise and I will meet some other day. There is no time now.

I get dressed and I'm gone.

I have left Zieg and Zieg II alone. I know my brother won't hurt the rat, Buddhist that he is. He may think the rat is our old aunt Ginny, which actually would make perfect sense. Zieg II has been hiding, coming out only to get his cheese and drink a little water, just like Auntie Ginny used to do. He has not recovered from the shock of seeing his former tormentor. Ginny thought every member of our family a tormentor of sorts.

Rats and aunts named Ginny—sometimes they know things the rest of the world doesn't.

■ ■ ■

Have you ever seen a depressed building? A building in want of tons of Prozac? The Chancecastle Publishing tower looks like a giant in the middle of menopause. Ground Zero in the near distance must be playing a trick on the neighborhood. Grouchy New York is now New York ready to throw itself from the Brooklyn Bridge. Something is wrong. Perhaps it's just my cellulite getting to my head. The building concierge, a plump woman in her sixties who keeps about sixteen cats in her apartment, is sweeping the hallway. Her customarily jovial face has fallen down like a basset hound's.

"Something the matter, Mrs. Beining?" I ask.

She produces a tear, which she wipes with the back of her hand.

"Oh, Miss Zimmerman," she says. "It's horrible! Just horrible!"

"I'm sorry," I say. "What's horrible?"

"I found her this morning. Bent over her desk. At first I thought she was asleep, you know. I told her many times she worked too hard. Staying at her office till the wee hours."

I let it all sink in. Mrs. Beining continues. She's on a roll. Her speech is a mad river, a stream running wild. She's making me dizzy. I hold my head, massage my temples.

"When I went to clean, I heard Barnaby growling, so I thought, how funny! Barnaby hardly ever growls, you know. A nice cat he is, too! Most people are scared of him, on account of him being...well...a bit wild. I take him for walks, you know, when Miss Chancecastle is too busy to have him out. I mean, when she was...Oh, it's too horrible...And now, now, what will happen to the poor cat?"

"Are you telling me that Agatha—that Ms. Chancecastle...had...some kind of heart attack?"

"Oh, no, Miss Zimmerman!" she says between tears and sniffs. "No, no! Like I said, at first it looked like she was asleep. But then I saw the blood. All the blood on her back. Someone shot her—or planted a knife there! I didn't look too close, you know. All the blood, I just couldn't take it."

Mrs. Beining takes a tissue from her pocket, dries her face, and then blows her nose.

"My God!" I mutter. "Agatha Christie, murdered!"

■ ■ ■

The concierge shakes me.

"Miss Zimmerman, Miss Zimmerman! Are you all right? Oh, dear! Let me make you some tea, honey, before you go upstairs and talk to the police."

"The police?"

"They're waiting for you. They have already talked to all of Miss Chancecastle's employees, except for that funny girl, what's her name? You know, the one who arrives even later than you. The cute girl with a face like a mouse. Ah yes, Nora. Nora isn't here yet."

In the elevator I just hang there like rag doll. After the ride I drag myself to my workstation. If they were doing a new version of *Night of the Living Dead*, I would be hired in a second. *"Zoe Zimmerman the new zombie. Zoe Zimmerman the new sensation!"* Or, as my parents would put it, *"Zoe Zimmerman the new zenzation as a zombie but wizout Ziegfried."* If they watch a movie, it's got to be *Zorro*, the one with Catherine Zeta-Jones. If they go to the zoo, they go right to the zebras. Zieg and I ate tons of zucchini when we were kids.

All around me at the office, faces are tight. The click of computer keys sounds like a military march. Every now and then, we turn our heads toward Donald Chancecastle's office. Donald was gracious enough to let police officers use his space. Strange, strange, I think. Donald doesn't like the police. He doesn't like to share his office. He doesn't like the law, cheats on taxes and on his wife, and is an aficionado of sexual harassment. His main targets are the newcomers and the interns. He had his hand on my waist once, another time on my butt. Now, when I see he's ready to confuse his hands with surgical paraphernalia, I glide away and go looking for my friend Lord Barney. The cat hates Donald. The mere sight of the man incites him to show his teeth. And when Lord Barney shows his teeth, it ain't exactly a Robert Redford smile. So whenever Donald is about to play Mr. Octopus with me, I have Lord Barney growling at my side. At that point, I'm showing my teeth, too. My grin would put the Sundance Kid's to shame. Donald grins back. But then he leaves. And then I pet Lord Barney, who licks my face.

Right now, Donald is nowhere to be seen. Neither is Lord Barney. I can't sit still. Pages of a manuscript titled *How to Pay Attention to God and Still Love Your Belly Button* are forming a small wall in my cubicle. Barricades of inanities that await my editing. When I'm done, the 550-page text will have shrunk to half its original size. Next is *Love Is in the Air, But Is the Air Polluted?* That one you'll have to read at the park while smoking a cigarette and making sure Mayor Bloomberg doesn't catch you.

Right now I cannot concentrate. All I can think about is a lonely lynx. What will happen to Lord Barney now that Agatha Christie is gone?

A midsize, barrel-shaped man in a three-piece suit comes out of Donald's office. A crown of Grecian Formula–dyed hair adorns the lower half of his head. The top is a desert, a surface so shiny that I am sure his wife confuses him with the furniture whenever she's dusting. It's flat, too; I want to invite my friends for a skating party there, or else use it as a mirror and tweeze my own mustache. I have other ideas about the use of this bald head, but the man's stern glance has a special beheading effect on my imagination. I massage my neck for a second. The man has a thick mustache, which he constantly touches and adjusts so that both sides form an even pagoda roof over his invisible mouth. And yet it is a mouth that smiles at me.

"Miss—" Pagoda-mustache removes a small notebook from his suit pocket. "Miss—ah yes—Miss Zimmerman," he reads. His voice is round like his figure; his manner of speaking is clean, articulate. He shows me to the entrance of Donald's office with a rather grand gesture. "Won't you come in?"

I enter. He follows, shakes my hand.

"I am Detective Leek. Hercules Leek."

He gestures to one of Donald's cushy chairs.

"Please sit down."

"I—"

"Is there a problem, Miss Zimmerman?"

"Well, yes."

He examines Donald's desk, taps his cheek with his index finger.

"Why don't you sit down and tell me about it," he says, his eyes still on the ebony desk.

"No."

"No?"

"I can't sit down."

"Why is that?"

"Lord Barney."

"Lord Barney?"

"Yes."

"You seem quite agitated, Miss Zimmerman."

How does Leek know? He's not looking at me; he's still examining Donald's ostentatious furniture.

"Who is Lord Barney?" Hercules Leek grins. "Your…uh…paramour, perhaps?"

"Yeah…of course not! Lord Barney is a cat. If I were a cat, I wouldn't mind having Lord Barney as a lover, though."

I do not add that, under such circumstances, I most definitely would be out of Zieg II's will. There is only so much you want to tell police, especially when it concerns rodents.

"Well, Miss Zimmerman, I like cats. But aren't there more pressing matters than feline issues right now?"

"Oh, I don't think so!"

Detective Leek rearranges the objects on Donald's desk. He straightens some papers, aligns the desk lamp with the statuette of a nude woman at the other end of the desk. He looks at the sculpture a little more carefully. The woman is standing, legs spread wide. The lasso she's holding in her right hand forms a halo of sorts on top of her head. I get it: The Octopus is into sainthood of a particular kind. The S and M kind. Leek moves the laptop to the center, and Ms. Sado-Maso Full of Grace a little more to the right.

"There," he says. He now turns to me. "Symmetry. It is very important, you know."

I examine Leek once more. The impeccable suit, the pressed shirt, the immaculate tie; the aristocratic bearing, the bonhomie, the slightly affected speech; the careful steps, the waxed shoes, the shiny head. The thick mustache that curves upward; the wide green eyes that can suddenly narrow and become blades. The weird obsession with symmetry.

Something isn't right here. For all I know, this Leek might have come straight from the loony bin. When was the last time you met a three piece suit, the NYPD and exquisite manners all wrapped up in the same package?

"May I see some ID, please?" I ask.

Leek smiles.

"You certainly may, miss."

He shows me his NYPD gold badge. It looks legit, but what do I know? I look at him suspiciously.

"I watch *Law and Order*," I say. "You don't fit the template."

He laughs. Of course he has teeth that, real or not, align along his gums in two even white lines. He looks at his watch.

"She should arrive any minute now."

"Who?"

"My partner." Leek slants his eyes, smiles again.

Great! I'll have two of them interrogating me. Although, frankly, this kind of reassures me. Two cops go more with the *Law & Order* arrangement. Let's see, we have Detective Leek. If we get someone like Detective Carrot, then the whole building will be healthy during the investigation.

"What is it you are smiling about, Miss—"

The door opens abruptly. A woman enters like the wind, holding a leash that connects to Barnaby.

I run to the cat, crouch to his level, hug him.

"Lord Barney!"

Lord Barney purrs, licks my cheek with his raspy tongue. Bye-bye, moisturizer.

"Say hello, Lord Barney!" Lord Barney gives me his paw. We shake hands. I hold the lynx's paw awhile longer. I see blood.

"I am afraid that is Terry Chancecastle's blood," the woman says. "I just got the lab reports back."

I know that voice.

"Well, how are you, Z-Z?"

Aimé is the only person I know from New York who calls me Z-Z. The other people who use that name all come from Noliar. I raise my head.

"Julie. Julie Hoffman!"

Julie and I have a whole childhood in common. Cat fights in common. Most of these took place in our favorite play field, Aunt Jane's fantastic house. There were Russian shawls spreading bright flowers on old tatty sofas, chairs that stood on uneven wood floors like wounded soldiers, and Julie's ass, or mine, that fell on occasion from these unstable chairs. Aunt Jane's plump, prune-wrinkled appearance only added to the pitching ship feel of her home. And yet that pitching ship was our zone of comfort.

Otherwise known as "Chainsaw Jane" because of her particular way of trimming trees, Aunt Jane did not believe in such radical intervention when it came to humans, at least when it came to Julie and me. She would let us resolve our own conflicts. A native of Russia and an enthusiastic, accented swearer, she'd tell us, "Pull each other's hair and become bold, and see if I *fooking* care! It's your goddamn *fooking* hair, and if you want to be as ugly as *fooking* sin, it's your *goddamn fooking* problem, girls." Without the constant regulation of our respective and intrusive mothers, and thanks to Aunt Jane's politics of *laissez-faire*, Julie and I learned survival and hair preservation.

During this "diplomatic" training in which, I must admit, Julie often had the upper hand, Jane would go back to her vodka (which she told us was water; but we had tasted her water), her Marlboros, and her funny cards. When we asked her what these were, she just said: "Tarot." The Tarot, she sometimes read to unfamiliar visitors. It's only later that we learned that Aunt Jane was a medium who worked for the NYPD. Julie and I were less shocked than the rest of the town. The Tarot, the visitors: we put two and two together. She was instrumental in helping Julie become who she was, a proud cop and a lesbian, two very challenging identities in a small conservative town like Noliar. I am sure Aunt Jane had something to do with Julie's decision to come to the city.

Julie was one of the cops in charge of the investigation when Marcel Pavie was arrested in Noliar. She's also partly responsible for getting Pavie out of jail. She looks the same. As slim as Leek is round, with a Sharon Stone face and celestial blue eyes. Two wrinkles put her tight mouth in parenthesis. She is in her concentration mode.

Oh boy!

15

"So what are you doing here, Z-Z?" Hoffman asks.

I pet Lord Barney.

"I was going to ask you the same thing."

She walks toward me.

"How about you letting me do the questioning this time?"

Leek produces a slight bow and pets his mustache.

"Why don't you sit down, Miss Zimmerman."

I want to say thanks, but no thanks. I want to get out of here, get out of the whole freaking situation. Pretend none of this ever happened.

I let my body fall on a chair, rub my face.

"So this isn't a dream. A bad dream."

"Afraid not," Hoffman replies.

"So where were you this morning before you came here, Z-Z?"

"Watching cellulite."

"Say what?"

I look at her athletic figure.

"Looks like you wouldn't know about that, Julie."

"Listen, Z-o-e," she articulates. I feel like a nine-year-old spelling bee contestant wearing a stupid dress crocheted by grandma and desperately in need of the nearest bathroom. "This is no time for jokes."

Maybe not. But fuck Julie for making that remark anyway. Thing is, I don't want to crumble. I don't want to scream. I hate these fucking banalities. You hear them spoken as lines in TV series and movies, and they don't mean a damn thing. It's just noise. What I want is to wrap myself in jokes, cover myself from top to bottom with *bons mots* or bad mots. What's funnier than facing cancer and a murder at the same time?

"Ha! Ha! Ha!"

Ouch! Someone has just slapped me. That would be Julie.

"Z-Z! Cut out your hysterics! Your behavior is—"

"Is what!"

"Well, odd."

"Odd?"

"Odd!"

"As in bizarre, strange, curious—odd?"

"As in throw away the thesaurus. You're not composing a goddamn poem, for Christ's sake."

Mm. I feel some kind of hostility directed toward poets here. Julie used to live with a poet. Are those two kaput? No longer singing the same verses?

As if I cared.

"Am I a suspect?" I ask.

"Everybody is a suspect, Miss Zimmerman," Leek says between mustache adjustments.

"But Julie knows me and—"

Leek comes close to me. There are blades in his green eyes.

"What do you mean, Miss Zimmerman?"

Hoffman crosses her arms, bites her lower lip.

"Well, Detective Leek, it's like this. Zoe and I used to play the same games, watch the same movies, listen to the same gossips yakking. Hide in the same places."

"Yeah. At Aunt Jane's house," I interject. "We love our Aunt Jane. Not really our aunt, but really she was better than our respective moms in so many ways. Tarot reader and vodka drinker extraordinaire. Better known as 'Chainsaw Jane.'" I chuckle, happy with both my portrayal and my disruption.

The two detectives look at each other.

"So I bet Zoe expects me to solemnly exonerate her from being a suspect," Julie continues after throwing me one of her special cop glances. "So, what do you say, Detective—why don't we just let her go? In fact, why don't we let all the Chancecastle employees go as well, since they are kinda-sorta connected to Zoe the Innocent?"

Well, not all of them, I want to tell her. There are a couple of macho jerks I wouldn't mind seeing behind bars. But for some reason, idiocy is still legal in this country.

"There are more pressing matters, after all," she adds. "This is just murder."

She doesn't have to be so sarcastic. I want to bite back. I want my response to be brilliant, a masterpiece of wit.

"You don't have to be so sarcastic!" I exclaim.

Julie grins.

"Bitch!" I mutter.

"I heard that," Julie says.

"Pff!" I reply with all the eloquence I can gather. "Pff!"

Lord Barney growls. I know exactly what he means.

Leek opens the door and sticks his head out into the hall.

"Officer Palmer, would you please come and take the cat away."

"No!" I shout.

"Miss Zimmerman, please!"

"I won't answer your questions if you take Lord Barney away!"

Julie takes a deep breath.

"It's all right, Detective Leek. She has a thing about cats and—"

I have a thing about rats, too. Should I tell her?

Leek stands erect by the door—a freaking barrel-shaped Doric column.

"I warn you, Miss Zimmerman. No more antics!" he says.

Once more, Lord Barney growls at Leek. I go to him, pet him, sit on the floor next to him. He places his head on my lap. It's beast and *moi*, together against the world.

"Lord Barney and I are ready for you," I declare. "Ask away!"

16

The MoMA is a desert. But I know he will be here. At this hour, the show is for my eyes only. Half of it is a retrospective. The abstract compositions that cover one wall have an aquatic feeling about them. I've never seen them before. I find them soothing. I catch myself smiling as I walk from one painting to the next. I walk to another wall. Masks painted against fiery backgrounds suddenly give me hot flashes. They stand proud and ready to move out of the paintings. It's the anger of Africa gliding through a whole panel of the museum. It seems fire was holding the brush, is still holding the brush. I tell myself that I have been a total ass. I have mismanaged my visit big-time. I should have gone to Pavie's hot masks first, and then to the aquatic compositions. I'd be feeling refreshed by now instead of like a menopausal maniac.

Marcel Pavie, aka Byron, who has been watching me examine his canvasses, comes over to me and fans me with a piece of paper.

"Are you cool enough now? Can I give you a hug?" he says with his ineradicable French accent.

I acquiesce and now I am in his arms.

"This feels good," I say.

I cling to him like an octopus. He laughs.

"Z-Z, you know we can't fuck."

"You mean you haven't converted yet?"

"Nope. Still as gay as the Follies Bergères."

"I don't blame you. I wouldn't fuck a straight guy if I didn't have to."

He laughs, throws his head back. Along with leopards, race horses, and the Lamborghini Diablo, he's probably one of the most gorgeous things I have ever seen. His lover Pete, now deceased, started calling him "Byron" because of his resemblance to Lord Byron, and then the nickname caught on with his other friends. After Pete's funeral, Byron made a series of gigantic portraits of his dead lover. Pete was not an attractive man, but the paintings are masterpieces.

Byron suddenly gives me a stern look. His brown eyes darken, his sensuous lips tighten. I take his hand, look at the range of chairs in the middle of the room.

"Aren't you tired of standing?" I tell him.

Byron wants to sit in front of the masks. Instead I lead him to chairs facing the aquatic paintings.

I say nothing for a while; I merely observe him. If only he were butter, I would spread him all over my tartines. My mind wanders; my feet tap against the floor.

"What?" he finally says.

"To think I can't even fantasize about you!"

He takes his glasses off, wipes them with the hem of his shirt, puts them back on. He now places his hand on my jittery legs. My legs stop; I sit still.

He gives me a Mona Lisa smile.

"I always had a thing for red hair."

"I've got a brother."

"I know your brother, Z-Z. He's a conformist. I don't do conformists." That mysterious smile again.

"Zieg threw conformism in the trash."

"You don't say! Did he leave his wife for a guy?"

"Close. He's gonna be a Buddhist monk."

"Good choice. That way, his robe and his hair will match."

My feet resume their staccato tap on the floor.

"Always the colorist, Byron. But when was the last time you saw the Dalai Lama with a pompadour?"

He pets my mane.

"What, darling?"

The woman who hasn't heard a French man say "darling" to her has something missing in her orgasms. I would seriously consider sharing my bed with him, with a dildo or a cucumber at my side for emergencies.

"You forgot about a Buddhist monk's hairdo." I perform a mock shaving gesture over my head.

"You could paint some of your masks on the back of their heads," I add.

"No, darling, with two faces they would have to enter politics."

I try to take a deep breath. But my yoga body has gone on vacation. My feet are still tapping the floor. My fingers are doing the moonwalk.

Byron takes my hands.

"What's the matter, Z-Z?"

"It's your best show, you know that."

"Changing the subject?"

"You don't think talking about your art is appropriate when we are sitting right in the middle of it?"

"You didn't come to talk to me about my art."

"How do you know?"

He looks at me.

"Is that a rhetorical question?"

"Do I look rhetorical?"

"It's written all over you."

"What's written all over me?"

His eyes are on an expedition. He's Cousteau with his *Calypso* and I am the fishy thing.

"Shit is written all over you," he finally declares.

He pronounces "shit" like "sheet."

"I wish!" I say.

"What?" he asks.

"I wish sheet were all over me. I haven't been sleeping very well lately."

He's still holding my hands, and his grasp and his glance get tighter.

"Stop it, Z-Z!"

My throat becomes knotty and my voice shakes when I speak.

"Well, it's true, Byron. I have hardly slept since—"

"Since?"

"I am going to lose it all, Byron. My job, my boob, everything!"

"Why are you holding your tears? Let them be."

"No!"

"Why?"

"Tears are so déjà fucking vu!"

"Right. And you wouldn't want déjà vu to fall all over you, would you?"

"Well, I have cried enough."

"Haven't we all?"

"I came to New York to stop crying."

"You picked the wrong city."

I keep silent. Déjà vu is wetting my face, and I need a Kleenex.

"What do you say we get out of here?" Byron suggests.

"And go where?" I ask.

Byron gets up, takes a tissue from his pocket, dries my face.

"The Bronx Zoo. Have you been there?"

Of course, this is the way to ask him. Why didn't I think of it?

"No," I lie.

As we exit the MoMA, I feel the masks burning my back. Byron is already on the sidewalk, watching the traffic. I turn toward the masks and give them the finger. I can only handle one type of anger at this point. Theirs can wait. I'll come and apologize later.

17

The day is cool, but the sun is bright, and after our visit to JungleWorld, Byron and I decide to have our hot dogs and popcorn outdoors. The terrace is pretty much ours. The table we choose is spattered with bird poop. Byron cleans it with one of his napkins. You would think the Bronx Zoo would have more exotic decorations.

"How long have you been a psychic?" I ask as I bite into my over-processed phallic symbol.

"What makes you say that?"

I wipe my mouth.

"Well, you knew my life was—how did you put it?"

"Shit."

"I knew that. I just love to hear you say it."

He raises one eyebrow.

"I read the papers."

"What?"

"That's how I know, Z-Z. I read the papers—not crystal balls."

I grab the mustard bottle. It's nearly empty. I press it as if my life depends on it. Sparkles of the yellow sauce reach Byron's face and glasses. No kidding, I have Jackson-Pollocked an artist.

"I am one of the suspects, can you believe it?"

Byron wipes his face with a napkin.

"Oh, definitely. You're one dangerous woman, especially with the Dijon."

The sun decides to hide behind a cloud. I feel a chill.

"You know," I continue, "I really liked Agatha Ch…Terry Chancecastle. I had no money in the bank when she gave me a job. I almost saw her as my guardian angel."

Byron cleans his glasses.

"Coming from an agnostic like you, it's interesting to hear you say that."

I give him a classified glance with no smile attached.

"As a matter of fact, the first time I met her was right here, at this zoo."

"So you have been here before," Byron interrupts. "Liar."

Damn! I should really think about indexing my lies.

"Never with you," I reply.

Byron is cutting his dog with a plastic fork and knife. His fancy silverware breaks at some point. He rises, glides away, grabs new utensils, glides back to the table. I want to tell him that he is not exactly having escargots here. But my mouth has to play dead for a while. I've got something to ask and I don't want to antagonize him.

"What are you going to do?" he asks.

"What am I supposed to do? I'm innocent!"

He suddenly becomes expressionless and that gives me the creeps. "I was innocent, too," he finally says.

"I am sorry. I forgot for a moment that the same thing happened to you."

"I was accused not of one but three murders, Z-Z. I—I went to prison."

"That was in a small town in PA. They didn't know any better. You were famous, you were French, and you were—"

"A fag," he says, completing my list.

"But this is New York."

On his fork is a perfectly sliced piece of hot dog and bun.

"And you are straight," he scoffs.

"Many straight people have twisted lives."

"Including you, Z-Z."

"Yup, I am a twisted straight. But I am hoping that the police in New York won't be as stupid as they were with you in dinky little Noliar."

Byron goes back to cleaning his bifocals. Finally he puts them back on.

"You should talk to a lawyer. Just in case."

"I am just a suspect."

"*Just* a suspect? Zoe, wake up! This is murder we are talking about!"

"Oh, yeah? How can I talk to a lawyer?"

"With your sharp mouth, of course, darling."

"Ha, ha, ha! So very funny! I mean, with what money? Donald Chancecastle gave me a week's notice. Come next week, I'm unemployed."

"You can make arrangements. I could help you." After a moment of silence, he adds, "What do you know about Donald Chancecastle?"

"That he's an ass! He's firing me. What do you mean? Have you heard anything?"

Byron doesn't answer. A long silence stretches.

"I have money, Z-Z. It's no problem," Byron finally says.

"You could throw it out the window for bums to grab, like you did in your younger days in LA." I try to smile.

"You knew about that?"

"Part of the Pavie legend. Tramps became Trumps because of you."

He nods distractedly. "You know powerful people can get away with murder. They treat the masses as a bunch of disposable, *framable*, insects. Do you understand what I am saying, Zoe? I know a couple of cases, one in L.A., one in Paris."

We look at each other for long seconds. I close my eyes and nod. Time to call a lawyer, I get it. I touch my breast again. Could I get a lawyer for my boob as well?

Byron breaks his fancy silverware again.

"Try the popcorn," I say.

Byron looks at what is now a demi–hot dog and then at the open trash can four feet away. His eyes trace the dog-can trajectory a couple of times. He then takes the emasculated thing, aims, and throws it perfectly into the can. He then wipes the tips of his fingers clean with a fresh napkin.

"Someone could take your case pro bono. The Chancecastle case is already making a lot of noise. It would be great publicity for a lawyer and his firm. You're going to be famous, Zoe."

I pick up the mustard again. Byron shields his face with his hands.

"Well, ain't that grand," I retort. "That's exactly how I wanted to have my fifteen freaking minutes, as a possible backstabber."

Byron's face brightens.

"I know! I know who can help you!"

I put down the mustard and give him a questioning stare.

"But of course! Farling, Joyce and Trenton. The firm. That's where you should go."

"Why should I go there?"

"Hello? Because of Clyde Trenton."

He sees my puzzled expression.

"Clyde Trenton, Marc Trenton's brother."

"Marc and I are history."

"Since when?"

"Since none of your business."

Byron raises his eyebrows and dusts his shirt off with the back of his hand. I am an annoying fungus at times, I know.

I get up.

"Let's walk."

"Again? Isn't it what we have been doing for the last two hours?"

"I have something to show you."

"About that lawyer," Byron insists.

"Let's change the subject."

"About that boob—"

"About your topics of conversation. You really know to pick them!"

"Well?" he insists.

"I told you. There's a strong possibility… chances are…God!" I touch my chest. "Chances are my boob's gotta…"

I can't finish the sentence. Byron takes my hand.

"Who's the surgeon?"

"Dr. Botox."

"Dr. Who?"

"Fontaine. Dr. Fontaine. Swollen ego, swollen cheeks."

"Swollen fees, too. I thought you had no money."

"You know him?" I ask. And then I realize how stupid my question is. "Of course. You made his portrait. No wonder his fees are high. He couldn't afford you otherwise."

"He handles the city's haute clientele. Millionaires. Either you won the lottery, or—"

"Or Marc was one of his students. One of his star students," I inform him.

"You just told me that Marc and you are kaput, fini."

"Yeah. But Marc was the one who found the lump in my breast."

"So he wants to follow through, right?"

"He has been following through without my knowledge. It's all pre-planned and prepaid, Byron."

"Looks like he still cares about you."

"Looks like he's got a doctor's ego. And male pride on top of it. Combine the two together, and it outswells Botox."

For a moment neither of us says anything.

"I don't think he told Dr. Fontaine we broke up," I say.

"Did you, really?"

"Did I really what?" I retort.

"Break up?"

I decide I'm done answering questions for the time being. I take Byron's arm. He kisses the top of my head. Any observer would think we were a well-established couple, seeing us walking like this. Maybe straight women should marry gay guys, and have the occasional affair on the side to avoid too many vagina monologues.

We stop in front of an exhibit.

"They've got beautiful snow leopards here," I say.

"Weren't we just here?"

"Maybe. But I wanted you to see them again."

"Why?"

"Well, one of my personal acquaintances is a lynx. A very nice cat who just lost his mom and—"

"Barnaby, right? Terry Chancecastle's pet. Oh…Oh, I get it! I get it! The reason you took me to this exhibit is to ask me to help Barnaby, isn't it? Even adopt him, perhaps?"

My mouth falls open. I stand there, paralyzed. If a photographer took my picture right now, he could title it "Portrait of an Idiot" and easily win first prize in a local art contest.

"How? But how—" I say eloquently.

"How do I know, Z-Z? Don't you read the papers? Your antics with Barnaby and the NYPD are all over the *New York Times*, the *Washington Post*, the *LA Times*—you name it. It's in every big paper, famous or infamous. Even the *Enquirer* wants to know, imagine that!"

18

It takes some time to convince Byron to take Lord Barney with him, especially when I tell him the reason I can't keep him myself is Zieg II the rat. He says he knows someone with a private jet who can transport him and Lord Barney without having to deal with regular police verification and other red-tape annoyances. Byron tells me he's going to take the cat to a Florida acquaintance who, he promises, loves cats, all sorts of cats. But I don't believe him. Not for a second. He's going to go stand with Lord Barney in front of the mirror, and he will see the beautiful tableau they make together and know on the spot that they are meant for each other.

I'm gonna miss Lord Barney. I'm going to miss hearing his eloquent growls. I'm especially going to miss watching the scared expressions of my coworkers when I walk him by their desks.

The way I see it, I did what I had to do.

It's a good thing the police have occasional moments of doughnut-filled inattention and that my colleagues are now burying themselves in their cubicles as if their lives depended on it. In no time, the cat and I are downstairs in Mrs. Beining's apartment. She agrees to hide Lord Barney until I can find him a good home. She realizes as well as I do that what we are doing is totally illegal. But she also knows what the law would do to Lord Barney by handing him over to Donald Chancecastle.

"He wouldn't even bother to bring him to the zoo," she declares.

"He would send him to the butcher and sell his meat to his posh friends, as a joke," I retort.

"You know, I should be scratched off that goddamn suspects list. Think about it," I add after a moment. "What these assholes at the NYPD don't get is that, had I decided to murder someone, I wouldn't have targeted the wrong sibling. The fat, larded one would have been easier to kill in more ways than one."

■ ■ ■

Police show up at Mrs. Beining's place to look for Lord Barney, but they leave empty-handed. How Mrs. Beining managed to keep him hidden, I don't know, although I suspect her sixteen other cats—some of them huge alley cats—as well as the aforementioned doughnuts, must have blurred their vision. After they have left, I wait for the concierge to call me. Just when I'm beginning to get really antsy, the phone rings. It's Mrs. Beining. The coast is clear, she tells me. Thanks to Aimé, Byron and I are at her door within minutes. Mrs. Beining is so enthralled by Byron's looks that I think she will not let him out. I observe her and in her eyes I see this question: Where is the leash for that new, exquisite, French creature? And then I see a bit of accounting: she is obviously rethinking her budget for additional bags of Friskies.

■ ■ ■

The deed is done. Now I can breathe, relax. But no, I feel dizzy. If I don't find my bed in a second, I am going to faint. I don't have to go far; my bed is right here. I fall on it. My entire body shakes. My breathing goes berserk. The room pitches in all directions. That's it, Zoe, I tell myself. That's it, you're going to look at the ceiling for an eternity, and the ceiling won't even stay still.

I try to take a deep breath, and then another, until I finally realize I can't do it. The breaths won't come. I am having a panic attack.

But I keep trying to breathe, and finally oxygen does its thing. The room decides to settle and tells the ceiling to do the same. Here I am, big hair, big mouth, smallish body and smaller budget, sharing space in a dinky apartment with a rat; here I am, in the midst of skyscrapers, sirens and solitudes; here I am, a woman escaping from pain and looking for fame in the Big Apple. Here I am, Zoe Zimmerman, lynx thief, murder suspect, and breast loser.

I want to laugh. And at first that's what I do. I laugh like a madwoman. Then the tears start. It's not Niagara Falls. It's a sweet, insistent rain. But my laughter has not totally ceased. It keeps drumming from within me like a stubborn echo.

Laughter and tears—it's rainbow time!

The laughter dies; the tears have won. They run out of me now like rain in a monsoon. I become a cascade. I become a kaleidoscope of palpitations. The warm, salty water is melting me away. I stay like this, drowned in this strange solace, for a period of time that seems elastic.

And then something tickles me. Hair. I open my eyes. No, can't be. I close my eyes, and it's tickle time again. I let my lids do their opening act once more. I now know with certainty that the tickler has been Zieg II's mustache. The rat managed to climb up onto my bed. How long he has been there, watching me, I don't know. But I manage a faint smile. I stretch my arms, I stretch my feet and toes, and I get up.

The mirror confronts me. I turn my back to it and then return to face it again. It's disfigured Zoe in there. Red skin, red eyes. Red hair. It's a bit overdone in my opinion. At least the red matches the bedroom color scheme and my brother's upcoming monk attire.

The doorbell rings. Zieg II stands on his back legs, twitches his mustache, looks left and right, scratches his nose to think about it, and then decides to leave the top of the bed to hide under it. The whole operation is completed in three seconds, cartoon rhythm. Of rats and men, I ponder. Then I drag myself to the door. Aimé.

"Did you lose your key again?" I ask.

He has a bag full of croissants in his hand, a newspaper under his arm.

"Sorry," he says as he enters. "I left it at my apartment."

He looks around.

"Your brother not here?"

"He went for a walk in the city."

"Ground Zero again?" Aimé asks.

I shrug.

"I don't know what he's looking for down there."

Aimé bends to give me a kiss, sees my face.

"Tu as pleuré. You have been crying?"

"No, red eyes and red faces are the new fashion. I wouldn't want to disappoint Donatella Versace or Pierre Cardin."

He places the croissants on the table.

"You read newspapers now?" I ask.

"Only when they talk about you," he grins. "Zoe is becoming a big star."

I take a tissue, blow my nose.

"If they could see me now!"

Aimé hugs me.

"It will all go away, Z-Z. You will see. Soon all of that shit will be gone."

Soon my boob will be gone, too.

"What does today's paper say?" I ask.

"You made first page."

"I—what!" I pull the *Times* from Aimé's underarm. First I see the photo Agatha Christie took of me in front of the lion exhibit. Right under it, there is an article, plus an editorial. I go for the editorial.

Zoe Zimmerman Prime Suspect in Lynx Disappearance.

Zoe Zimmerman, an editor at Chancecastle Publishing, has recently become the prime suspect in the disappearance of Barnaby, the pet lynx of Terry Chancecastle, the company's late CEO. Ms. Chancecastle was found stabbed to death in her office on February 9 by Brenda Beining, the head concierge at the Chancecastle building. Forensics believe that the murder occurred during the night of

February 8, between 10 and midnight. Although most employees, including Donald Chancecastle, Terry Chancecastle's brother and the publishing company's second in command, are still under suspicion, Zoe Zimmerman's antics have made the police nervous and somewhat apprehensive. During her initial police questioning, Zimmerman kept asking for "Lord Barney," Zimmerman's pet name for Barnaby.

Zimmerman also had a special name for Terry Chancecastle. Other editors heard her refer to the CEO as "Agatha Christie." While many at the company thought Ms. Chancecastle's resemblance to the famous mystery writer was discernible, many also thought that a powerful publisher wouldn't have tolerated being nicknamed thus by a low-level employee had there not been some type of familiarity between the two women. When told of Chancecastle's death, Zimmerman exclaimed, "Agatha Christie, murdered!" Beining reported to the press.

Zimmerman is allegedly sharing her apartment with a rat. A source who wishes to remain anonymous told the Times *that Zimmerman was recently diagnosed with breast cancer. The source wondered if the diagnosis might have been a catalyst for Zimmerman's eccentricity in her dealings with her coworkers and the police.*

A native of Noliar, a small town in Western Pennsylvania, Zimmerman moved to New York five months ago in the hope of becoming a published novelist. A source told the press that one of her bathroom walls is plastered with rejection slips. "Some of them fall into the commode and they flush pretty well," she allegedly told the source. Zimmerman has been working at Chancecastle Publishing for the past eight weeks, but she and Terry Chancecastle had met prior to Zimmerman's employment at the company. Catherine Brokaw, who has been with Chancecastle Publishing for the past twenty-one years, told police that long before Zimmerman was hired by the megapublisher, she saw a photo of Zimmerman on Chancecastle's desk. Terry Chancecastle allegedly made comments to Brokaw about the picture. "Miss Chancecastle thought Zoe looked like a lion, with her big red hair and all. So she took that picture of her in front of the lion exhibit.

And then Miss Chancecastle placed the picture in an envelope, wrote Zoe's address on it, and asked me to mail it," Brokaw stated. Other employees also knew of the photo. Says CP editor Lilian Rather, "Maybe it's because Zoe looks like a lion that she likes Barnaby so much. And maybe she's fierce like all these wild cats, you know. Maybe she got mad one day and killed Miss Chancecastle." Like Zimmerman, Brokaw, Rather, and the other Chancecastle employees are still under suspicion.

Zimmerman insists she met Chancecastle at the Bronx Zoo at the time the picture was taken, and that finding a job at Chancecastle Publishing was "pure coincidence." The statements of several editors at Chancecastle Publishing, including Albert Canich, Thomas Martinez, and Jeffrey Brukowski, seem to challenge Zimmerman's claim. "Everybody was afraid of Barnaby," Brukowski said. "I mean, everybody. I've been here for eleven years, so I know. And then Zoe Zimmerman arrives and she pets the lynx as if he were a French Poodle. And I think something is wrong with that picture."

Chancecastle employees' reactions to the lynx's disappearance have been mixed and clearly divided between male and female employees. Albeit saddened by Chancecastle's death, most male editors admit being somewhat relieved at Barnaby's departure. The female employees who spoke to the Times expressed concern for the lynx. Interestingly, Zimmerman, who had developed a close relationship with the feline, did not display any form of worry or concern. When asked about it, Zimmerman answered, "I tried the heart-on-the-sleeve thing. But I consider it a fashion faux-pas. Then I tried it on a hat. That doesn't work, either. So usually I just stuff it inside where no one can see it."

New York's mayor has sent extra patrol officers to search the city streets and subway stations for the missing animal. "Our tax money is being spent on a search for a lynx. What next?" one New Yorker complained.

Detectives Julie Hoffman and Hercules Leek of the NYPD are in charge of the investigation of Terry Chancecastle's murder. Leek has told the press that there is no particular prime suspect at this point, and that the inquiry will go on until the killer is apprehended. To this, Detective Hoffman added, "Whom will this murder benefit? That's the basic question, isn't it? You figure it out and let me know!" Hoffman is a native of Noliar and one of Zimmerman's former schoolmates.

Whom will this murder benefit, indeed? The logical response would be Donald Chancecastle, who now has total control of Chancecastle Publishing. According to sources at the company, Mr. Chancecastle has begun making cutbacks in personnel, and Ms. Zimmerman was among the group of employees let go. Benefits have been reduced as well. Says Mr. Chancecastle, "I loved my sister and am certainly grieving over her sudden and tragic death. But I have to do what's best for the company. Terry was a great CEO but perhaps a bit of an idealist. With these harsh economic times it is necessary to put aside idealism and apply more realism to the situation."

Terry Chancecastle was also a complex and rather secretive person. An anonymous source told this reporter that Ms. Chancecastle left a substantial sum to the Bronx Zoo for the purpose of expanding and improving the facility's lion exhibit. Does this connect to Zoe Zimmerman, who was compared to a lion by Chancecastle? A framed copy of the photo of Zimmerman standing in front of the lions' stand was found in Terry Chancecastle's apartment. The Times obtained permission from Donald Chancecastle to publish the photo.

Right now, a lynx may well be walking the streets of New York. Several commuters have informed police that they saw "a large cat" in the subway. It has since been verified that the animal in question is an alley cat named Eugene who apparently resides in the subway. Henry Woods and Cindy Sibble, two homeless people and frequent residents of the subway, say that the multitude of rodents living underground explains the size of Eugene. "In fact, there are doubtless a great many Eugenes living in the subway," Dr. Hernandeze told the Times, "and that's a good thing. We should be thankful to Eugene and his fellow felines for helping us control the rat population in the city." As to whether Barnaby is wandering

somewhere in Manhattan or being hidden by a human friend, per-
haps we should ask Zoe Zimmerman.
        V. M.

Nice piece of writing, I think, before everything starts to move around
me like before: the walls, the floor, the furniture. I fall into a chair. Aimé
comes to massage my shoulders.

"Z-Z, I am sorry. Maybe I don't show you the paper anymore."

I hold his hand.

"Right! And then people would have looked at me funny and—"

"People look at you funny anyway," a deep voice interrupts.

I look up.

"When did you get in?" I ask my brother who, like Aimé moments
ago, is holding a paper.

"Another copy of the *Times*. I guess we should frame the article now."

The cranky house phone rings.

"I'll get it!" Zieg says, his voice muted—a buried grotto. He picks up
the receiver in his usual nonchalant way. No matter how big the drama,
Zieg usually maintains a calm composure. He made a tabula rasa of his
past, went through a little death, but has kept his relaxed manner of speaking and his aplomb. If you ask me, his calm isn't the result of transcendental meditation; I think it's pure macho bullshit. Repress, repress, repress.
Deny, deny, deny. Mess up Kubler-Ross's list just for the hell of it.

"Uh-huh...Uh-huh...Uh-huh," Zieg sounds like some annoyed cow
now. After a few more moos, he hands the phone to me. "It's Mom."

Mom. I owe her a few phone calls and a few letters. But I'm not up
for talking with her right this moment. I know why her crisp little voice is
standing by.

I hand him back the phone.

"Tell her it's a bunch of fucking lies."

Zieg covers the talking part of the receiver with his hand.

"Why won't you speak to her?"

"She's the Wall of Lamentations all by herself! And when she doesn't
lament, she bites. She's gonna tell me I am in trouble and—"

"But you *are* in trouble, Zoe!"

"Great!" Aimé mumbles. "That's what Z-Z needs to hear right now."

"Hello? Hello? Ziegfried…Zoe…are you there? Hello?" A mix of chirping and crackling sounds comes from the phone. The chirping is my mom. She talks like a bird, eats like a bird, and has a sharp biting beak. The crackling, I figure, is Mom modernized with a cell phone.

"Mother, I—" Zieg starts. "Mother, it's like this—"

It's going to take an eternity for Zieg and his cavernous voice to explain things. I pull the phone out of Zieg's hand.

"Hey, that hurts!" he yells.

"Poor baby!" I declare. "I didn't pull your teeth out!"

"Thank God you're not a dentist!"

I turn my back to Zieg, address a crisp smile to Aimé, who is now sitting on the couch reading the *New York Times*. Page one is on the floor and his foot is right on it. I wonder if Lord Barney and I should feel relieved or insulted to have our story, no matter how distorted, stepped on like this. And then Zieg II comes in to inquire. He steps on the page, circles around it, goes to chew one corner, spits the paper out, and runs away. Looks like the *Times* is not the rat's cup of tea.

"Hello? Zoe…Ziegfried…are you there? Hello?"

"Mom! Long time no see! So what's new? Looks like you got a cell phone. Well, congrats, mom!" I tell the receiver.

"Did you read the article about you in the *Noliar News*?" the chirpy receiver replies.

"Well, *le tout* New York reads the *Noliar News*, Mom, but I guess I missed today's edition.

"Lara Clement…you remember Lara Clement?"

"Noliar's gossip-in-chief?"

"She's not a gossip. She just talks."

I raise my eyes to the ceiling's major crack.

"OK. She just talks. What did she just talk to you about?"

"She read an article about you in the *Pittsburgh Post-Gazette*. So they talk about you in the city, too."

I massage my forehead.

"Well, Mom, you've got a famous daughter, what do you say to that?"

"What do I say to that?" the voice twitters at the other end. "What do I say to that? Well, Zoe, I say, wonderful! Fabulous, just fabulous! I have a daughter suspected of murdering a CEO, of kidnaping a lynx, of looking like a lion, and of living with a rat. It's going to do wonders for my reputation."

"Well, Mom, I—"

"On top of that, she has breast cancer. And does she pick up the phone to share that with her mother? Of course not. That's too damn trivial, I guess!"

I grind my teeth.

"If I do say so myself."

"Zoe, you left Noliar and all hell broke loose. New York is no good for you. Come back. You'll have a nice life again here, just like before."

I place the phone in front of me, observe it as if it were an odd statue. And then I do something I am not particularly proud of. I make a fist with my free hand and punch its upper part. Damn, it hurts. I bring the phone back to my ear.

"Sure, Mom. I had a lovely life in Noliar. Just lovely!"

"Nice friends, too."

"Absolutely. Why would I leave such a paradise?"

"Don't be sarcastic. Noliar is as good a place as any. With good doctors. Just as good as the ones in New York, I bet. Do you know Dr. Trenton comes here sometimes and asks about you?"

"Marc Trenton was not my attending doctor, Mom."

Silence at the other end.

"He was the married doctor I fucked, Mother." I feel satisfied that I have just given Mom the coup de grace. A smile spreads like a cut across my face.

"Well, we all know he can't fuck his wife."

I see that when my mother updated her life with a cell phone, she updated her vocabulary as well. So much for my coup de grace.

I lean against the wall.

"How—how did you know?"

"Everybody knows the doctor's wife sleeps with other women."

"But they had a child together, Mom."

"Well, dear, many women want to have children," Mom says. "Many. A great majority, in fact. I wish you were part of that majority."

I place the phone in front of me again and try to counterfeit as best as I can a demonic smile. I am unsuccessful. From the glances Aimé and Zieg send me right now, I imagine I look like an idiot. A career as the devil is not for me. I give the phone the finger. That, I can do.

"Don't tell me you didn't know?" Mom asks.

"Zieg told me. But who can believe an ex-geek about to become a Tibetan monk?"

Silence blankets the apartment all of a sudden. It won't last. Mom tears it apart.

"I've lost my children. Jesus, Mary, and Joseph, what have I done to you two to deserve this?"

I know a full-fledged litany is about to fly out of the receiver. So I click my fingers. One, two, three, four! Here it comes, right on time.

"I mean, I don't know what's worse. A daughter about to go to jail with only one breast, or a son about to go to Tibet with no hair and a red toga! There has never been a mental case in my family. Never! But now look what's happening! Look what's happening! A son about to twist his body and his soul with silly yoga postures, and a daughter who loves cats and lives with a rat. What is happening to this world, Lord Almighty? What is happening to me? I never should have married a Jew. I should have listened to my mama. Mix religions in the same bed, and you never know what the results are going to be. That's what she told me, but I didn't listen to her. I should have married a nice Catholic man. I knew one back then, one who really wanted me. He was ugly as sin, poor boy, but I should have picked him. I might have had ugly children, but at least they would be sane. Sane. Instead I picked your father. Of course, he's good looking, but that's about it. When I told him about you going to New York City, you know what he said? 'Let her be,' he said. Imagine!

And when your brother went crazy and decided to go Buddhist? 'Let him be.' That's all he can say. Oh, yes, I should have married that ugly Catholic boy. I had the chance of a lifetime there, a real opportunity. And I missed it!"

19

Aimé tells me to think about a lawyer. Zieg tells me he won't leave for Tibet until I get a lawyer. Byron reads about me in the *LA Times*, calls me, and insists, "Darling, have you hired a lawyer yet?" And then there are the other phone calls. The urgent messages with the sensuous voice. "Zoe, it's Marc. Please pick up…please…OK, don't. But listen…I talked to my brother. He's one of the best criminal attorneys. And…well…there are very powerful people around you. People who can crush you, Zoe. This Donald Chancecastle, I wouldn't trust him. And the press. Look at what the press is doing with your story. Please talk to Clyde. He says he'll take your case pro bono. And you have an appointment with Dr. Fontaine. Please don't forget, Zoe!"

My heart behaves as if it's training for the world championship of boxing. I tell it to cool it, just cool it. But it ignores me; it keeps punching away.

"Why didn't I erase this message like I did with the others, eh, Ziggy?"

The rat looks at me and twitches his whiskers.

"It's nice to be alone, isn't it? Just the two of us."

I suspect that, at the moment, Aimé is sliding his cab between angry vehicles, doing questionably smooth zigzags, and scaring his clientele half to death. As for Zieg, he's perambulating throughout the city, doing his premeditation. That is, meditation before hair deletion and robe addition.

The sun comes into the kitchen with accusatory fingers. It reveals a linoleum floor in need of urgent care from Dr. Clorox. I open the window. Some people lift weights to work out their arms. No need for dumbbells here. All I have to do is open the kitchen window. Every attempt makes me wonder whether or not the glass is going to break. It vibrates, coughs like an old man, resists like an insurgent. I feel like a dentist pulling out a superglued molar. Either the construction worker and the window maker did not know about measurements, or they were on acid during the whole process. Finally the window opens. Particles of dust fly into the kitchen, making a miniature version of the Milky Way in the shafts of light that stream down to the dirty floor. They'll be able to twinkle long before I pick up a broom. I smell the outside air. It slaps my face. Spring is coming with a bite. I hug myself, look down at the floor.

"Yup, it's just you and me, Ziggy. I've lost my job, I'm about to lose my breast, and I've gained some kind of a reputation. Two losses, one questionable gain, each one of them the cause of a major headache. But this morning, I've decided, I am going to take it easy. A few hours without worries, without lovers, without brothers. Just moments spent alone with a rat. I need it. I really need it, Ziggy."

Have I lost my mind? That's what Ziggy's tiny little black eyes tell me.

"You want some cheese, don't you?"

Ziggy stands on his back legs, and scratches his mustache, excitedly. I decode the posture: I have now recovered my senses!

I go to the fridge. On top of it I see the vase. The vase that held Marc's last bouquet. I push it back against the wall, place a big box of cereal in front of it.

When I give the cheese to Ziggy, he looks at me as if I have betrayed him, big-time.

"Sorry, mozzarella again," I say.

Ring-ring. Fucking phone.

"Hello?"

"Zoe Zimmerman? Hi, I'm calling from the *National Enquirer.* We would like to do an interview with you and—"

"Wrong number." As soon as I hang up, the phone rings again. "Let it be, let it be," I sing and walk away. I let the answering machine do its job. The voice that erupts from the tinny speaker comes from a man who must have eaten the world's supply of sausages and smoked most of Castro's cigars. Think Henry Kissinger, only with a full-blown Pittsburgh accent.

"Hello, this is Clyde Trenton, from Farling, Joyce and Trenton. This message is for Zoe Zimmerman. Would you please give me a call back at—"

Damn! Where did my special moment with the rat go? I pick up.

"Hi. This is Zoe Zimmerman."

"Well, hello, Miss Zimmerman."

"Zoe."

"Well, Zoe, I have—mm—I have read about you. Let me cut to the chase. You are in a difficult legal situation. It looks like you need a lawyer, dear."

"Not dear. Zoe," I make a face at the phone. Yes, I may need a powerful lawyer at this point in my life, but I've had it up to here with guys treating me like a goddamn little girl. I raise my middle finger.

"Well, Zoe, what do you say we make an appointment, you and I?" the Yankee Kissinger ejaculates.

I want to cut this conversation short with a sharp blade. The voice I hear at the other end is about to give me indigestion. But I play dumb.

"An appointment?"

"I am a criminal defense attorney, Zoe. Quite a good one, in fact." The man's tone is impatient now, sizzling like hot grease.

"Well, Mr. Trento—"

"Clyde—"

Touché.

"I am just a writer, Clyde. Not a criminal."

"It looks like you have powerful enemies, Zoe."

"Again, I am *just* a writer."

"Well, powerful people can make criminals out of 'just writers,' as you put it."

"What? What the hell do you mean?"

"What type of writing do you do, Zoe?"

"Uh…fiction. Kinda innocent, don't you think?"

Clyde chuckles. "Mm. Listen. Powerful people can transform fiction into reality. Power, and a minimum of grey cells, will do the trick. If they want the guilt to fall on some people less powerful than they are, they will—how shall I put it—*invent* a criminal. They will pay corrupt cops and officials. And, my dear—I mean Zoe—you have been acting strangely lately. You are the perfect target. So I'd say you definitely need a lawyer."

"I can't afford you."

"You shouldn't worry about that. It's taken care of."

"Am I a charity case?"

"Charity, my dear—excuse me, Zoe?" Trenton produces a chuckle that reminds me of someone who has eaten too many frijoles in one sitting. "Do you think I practice charity?"

"You're a good brother, then. Marc convinced you to take my freaking case."

"Even if Marc had not spoken to me, I would have called you. You're quite a fascinating case, you know that? And representing you is not going to hurt the firm. Au contraire. So how about that appointment?"

■ ■ ■

I have not had my breakfast yet but, right now, I do not feel particularly hungry. I think of Clyde Trenton, his nasal speech. The man has been in New York City for years now, but never lost his Western Pennsylvania accent. Marc doesn't have it; I don't have it. I wonder if it's nostalgia that makes some people keep their accents despite the time spent away from their native corner. Some linguistics experts claim it's due to fossilization in the language-acquisition areas of the brain.

A chill creeps into the apartment. I realize that the kitchen window is still open. I try to push it down. But it won't close. I go to the couch, look underneath, and find the hammer there. I hit each corner of the window frame three times. It finally goes down and settles into its receptacle. I have locked a box, liberated more dust. This time, it comes without a sparkle. The sun has gone away. So has the rat. A piece of mozzarella remains untouched on the floor.

Ziggy is on a hunger strike.

On top of everything else, I have a spoiled rat on my hands.

20

On Central Park West, between Seventy-Third and Seventy-Fourth, the Hal N. Glam Building stands stout and square, self-assured, and full of it. From where I am now, fifty yards away from the building and close to the park, to trees and winding paths and statues coated in pigeon shit, the windows that pierce the whitish brick exterior look like a division of beady eyes. Two small pyramids planted on either side of the roof serve as astounded eyebrows. A few drivers slam on their brakes when I cross the street. The sudden, raspy squeak of rubber against asphalt incites pigeons to seek a new crumb-picking address. I am in the middle of the street. I have with me a large, ancient black umbrella—one of my father's rejects and my brother's recently discovered self-defense device. With the umbrella in hand, I feel invincible. A symphony of honks accompanies my little sidewalk-to-sidewalk stroll. Fingers stick up from hands stuck out of car windows. A white SUV stops ten inches from me.

"We've just met, buddy. We're not even casual acquaintances. Keep your distance, will ya?" I say, hoping the driver of this pretentious tank will read my lips.

The driver ejaculates words that may or may not recognize themselves in the latest revised edition of *Merriam-Webster.* I have just a second to indent the gleaming vehicle with the tip of my umbrella without being noticed. There! A nice little black line, with twists and turns in its own right, and that, I figure, won't disappear for less than one or two hundred bucks. I walk tall.

"Hey, lady, didn't your mama teach you to cross the fucking street?" a man in a battered Honda Civic yells.

"And your papa, didn't he teach you to paint cars, you rust-loving moron?"

Chic avenue, chic car, chic exchange. I love New York!

Finally I reach the other side. A man built like a balloon walking his Chihuahua and a woman built like a twisted wire walking her Doberman cross my path. They seem oblivious to the fact that the dogs are discussing major issues and barking out an argument. The Chihuahua is winning. Downcast, the Doberman poops on the sidewalk. Then His Roundness steps in the poop, to the great embarrassment of Her Wireness. They start their own argument now. The dogs take sides. I move on.

The double-height entrance, painted black and gold, gives the Hal N. Glam Building the air of a plump old lady about to go to a soiree. On top of it a golden plaque glimmers with *nouveau riche* satisfaction. Imposing and polished to a gleam, engraved between two rococo brackets, the firm proclaims itself to all who enter: Farling, Joyce and Trenton, LLP. I count the steps that lead to the grand entrance. Five. When I push the door, my arms start to ache. I wonder if there was a lead surplus when Glam built the nine-story structure, or if Richard Simmons gave ideas to the architect in order to tone the biceps of rich New Yorkers. Now I am in a red-carpeted foyer that leads to another door, this one automatic. More red carpet, an ocean of it. It's a good thing I have in my hand Daddy's diseased old umbrella. With it I duplicate Moses's famous gesture. If the Farling, Joyce and Trenton red-and-pure-wool sea splits in half, what will I find underneath?

A voice interrupts my Biblical pantomimes.

"May I help you, ma'am?"

The receptionist wears a dark miniskirt over well-toned legs, a pink sweater over a 34D bust, a crisp smile, a loose blond chignon, and a vacuous gaze with a voice to match. I don't know who Xeroxed Britney Spears, but there she is.

"This is our special clients' salon," she recites as she shows me a plush corner on the right. "Won't you please sit down?"

No waiting room, a "salon." I let my umbrella point to the mingling of brown-leather club armchairs and side tables; the Queen Anne coffee table where an array of magazines is spread like a señorita's fan; the curio china cabinet filled with fragile objects d'art; the Oriental rug, the striped beige-and-white wallpaper.

"May I take your...uh...umbrella?" the Britney-Spears analogue asks nervously.

I pet the disjointed black thing.

"Be careful, honey, it's an antique."

Blondie appears doubtful.

"Maybe," I say as the rusty end of the umbrella taps onto the glass of the china cabinet, "we should put it right here. It will go wonderfully with everything else."

"Oh, no!" she exclaims. She then swiftly removes the umbrella from my hand.

"What's in the armoire?" I ask, just noticing the massive, dark wood structure. One of my former below-the-belt acquaintances dealt in antiques. An armoire just like this one, with sculpted squares and the smell of encaustic, sat in his shop. He opened it for me, and showed me lavender sachets he had placed on its shelves. "Eighteenth-century provençal," he'd declared as I smelled the sachets.

I wonder if there are similar sachets inside this one. I have the urge to open it, to smell lavender, to get lost in a lovely scent for just one minute.

"So what's in the armoire, Britney?"

"My name is not Britney. It's Doris."

"Ah. Much better," I say. Whaddya know, her name matches the furniture. "Can I see inside?"

"Damn! Damn! Damn!"

Doris and I both turn our heads to see what kind of creature goes with the furious voice. It's a suit and tie with thick blond hair and an Aryan face. About thirty-two, with a body that suggests regular use of a gym membership. He swings his attaché case, lets it drop on the floor, makes a fist with his left hand and then with his right, and repeats, *"Damn!"*

"Excuse me," Doris tells me. She walks toward him. He fondles her butt. She removes his hand from her anatomy and then hits it with my umbrella. I feel so proud of owning such a useful device. Doris then throws a dry glance at Mr. Sexual Harassment.

"You're late, Frank. Your client has been waiting in your office for over twenty minutes."

"I am not up to seeing clients now!" he declares.

"You've got no choice," she says.

"Give me a kiss first, little Doris!"

"Kiss my ass, Frank. Oh, that's right, you don't kiss ass, you just pet ass without permission."

"I can do that; you're the receptionist."

"Have been for five years, Frank. Five years. You've been here for three months and you think you own the place, you fondling fascist!"

"Looks like I may have misjudged Doris. As for Frank, men like him come a million in a million. Every syllable of their argument comes to me sharp and clean. The acoustics in this place are terrific.

"Please be nice, Doris! Do you know what happened to me today?"

"No, and I don't want to know!"

"Well, I got a dent in my brand-new SUV, that's what I got! And I'm pretty sure who did it, too!"

Doris smiles. She seems genuinely happy.

"Who?"

"A bitch who crossed the street without looking! In fact, I bet it's her! She was walking with an umbrella."

"OK, just so we're clear, let's review your case. The weather forecast said there would be showers today, and the sky looks like lead. The woman you think dinged your car was walking with an umbrella, and the woman sitting over there came in with an umbrella. Therefore, she dinged your car. Why, Frank, your deductive skills are astonishing."

"It's her. She used the damn umbrella to dent my car. It was a bitch with big red hair exactly like hers."

Frank continues his monologue as Doris quickly places my umbrella behind the reception desk. Obviously, Frank is too absorbed with Doris's bottom, Doris's bosom, his own navel, and his SUV to notice what could be construed as hard evidence. Doris looks at me, sends me a broad grin.

"Frank, go see your client now. Otherwise, I'll report you to Clyde."

"Fine," he mumbles as he calls for the elevator.

The elevator opens its doors and swallows up the umbrella victim.

Doris returns with a key.

"Cognac. That's what's in the armoire," she announces.

She unlocks the armoire, finds the liqueur, fills a potbellied glass with it.

"Here," she says as she hands it to me.

21

"Am I going to be arrested?"

"Arrested? I don't think so. It's all circumstantial."

"Then why do I need you?"

Clyde's monumental frame rests on the edge of his monumental mahogany desk. Unlike the waiting room, which gives the impression of a bric-a-brac collection assembled by wealth rather than design, Clyde and his desk are in total harmony with each other. It is dark brown; Clyde wears a brown suit, a brown mustache, and has yellow teeth. Now he bends over me, opens his mouth. Where are my Altoids? I'm no clairvoyant, but I can tell he had fries and a steak with barbecue sauce less than thirty minutes ago.

He rubs his hands.

"Why do you need me? Well, Zoe, we don't want to you to be arrested, do we?"

"You just said—"

"You won't be arrested," he interrupts, "because you have hired me. I won't let that happen, you see."

"You mentioned circumstantial evidence." I am feeling dizzy, ready to fall asleep on the oversized armchair. I shouldn't have let Doris give me another cognac. The girl filled my glass to the rim both times, as if it were wine. I make a serious effort to listen to what Clyde is saying. But now and then, all

I can hear is the sound of his voice. It reminds me of the roaring of a train, with a faint background noise—a blend of snoring and fly buzzing. I mentally slap my face. I have to forget about the sound and listen to the words.

"Rich people," Clyde continues, "can transform circumstantial evidence into hard evidence."

"How?" I ask, my lids half-open.

"By hiring lawyers gifted with twisted reasoning and a lot of imagination. Top lawyers."

"So top lawyers are like top fiction writers?"

"Pretty much. Journalists, too, by the way. Look what they've done to you in the press."

In my cognac-induced torpor, it dawns on me that Clyde does not resemble his brother Marc in the least. Except for that inquiring flicker in the blue eyes. Clyde's enormous face widens at the cheeks and traces hills and valleys that only a tourist lacking an X chromosome would want to visit. In the middle of it is the nose of a tired Santa Claus, its tip reddened by things other than cold and snow—cognac and bourbon would be my guess. The suit that covers this creature is expensive, but he might as well be wearing a suit from Kmart. The folds and creases in the fabric build around him like fault lines on a volcano.

"That's what I am, you know, a fiction writer," I say with a dragging voice that would put to shame the proudest of drunks.

"Yes, you already said that on the phone. You're a writer, not a criminal. They're not synonyms. I got that."

"Well, I could help you with the fiction part of my defense, how about that?" The cognac makes me feel lethargic, yet brilliant.

"We can see about that later," Clyde says. "Now, let's talk about facts."

"No fiction?" I am disappointed.

"No fiction for now. Where is Barnaby?"

"Lord Barney? I came here to talk to you about Lord Barney?"

"In part, yes."

"I don't know. I don't know where Lord Barney is."

"OK now, Zoe. Rule number one, you must tell your lawyer the truth. I need to be prepared in case the other side finds out."

"Finds out what?"

I see impatience in his gaze. He twists his head like a turtle, grabs the phone, and pushes a button.

"Bonnie, would you come in here, please?"

"Hee, hee!" I laugh.

"How much cognac did Doris give you?" Clyde's air is somber.

"Two. Filled to the rim. Hee, hee, hee!"

"Filled to the rim? But with cognac you only fill the bottom of...How often do you drink cognac?"

"Never. I don't—I don't d-d-drink. But the stuff is *gooood*! Really, really *gooood*! I am seriously considering a career as an alcoholic."

He zooms in on me with a dissecting stare.

"Well, Zoe, what's so funny?"

"Your colleague, Bonnie."

"Bonnie is funny?"

"Bonnie...and Clyde. I've got lawyers called Bonnie and Clyde!"

"Oh, boy!"

Clyde presses another button.

"Doris, bring some coffee this way, please. And a cold compress if you can. And, sweetheart, remind me to show you the proper way to serve cognac."

■ ■ ■

I am now coffeed up. The compress Doris brought feels comfortable laying across my forehead. Maybe I'll start wearing compresses at home. Clyde swallows two aspirins and hands me two, which I wash down with what's left of my third cup of coffee. The compress falls. I pick it up, place it on the arm of my chair.

Bonnie comes into the room. Her plump body is armored in a narrow business suit; her dark hair frames her round face like a helmet. She shakes my hand, gives me a quick "Bonnie-Farling-nice-to-meet-you" before handing a file to Clyde. She then takes the chair next to mine.

Clyde opens the file and flips through its pages.

"Ready to go on now?"

I shrug my shoulders.

"If you insist."

"So where is Barnaby?"

I add a little bit of sugar to what's left of my coffee, and swallow the bittersweet liquid. Then I finally speak.

"I need to go to the powder room."

"Now? Haven't we wasted enough time?" Clyde is obviously not bathing in Nirvana.

"I really need to go," I say.

Clyde produces a rictus that cuts his face in half. The smile of a hippo about to cut a crocodile in half appears in my mind.

"You're doing that on purpose, aren't you," he says.

"Clyde!" Bonnie interjects in a firm tone.

"What?"

Bonnie glances sternly at her colleague.

"Two huge cognacs and three coffees. I believe her when she says she needs to use the restroom." She then turns to me. "The restroom is three doors down on the left."

It's only when I return that I notice a Pavie painting right above Clyde. A recent piece. Part of his masks series—although one I have not seen before. I must admit, it's stunning in a scary way. And it's looking right at me with accusatory eyes. It looks like it knows I gave the finger to its colleagues at the MoMA. I decide to confess.

"Lord Barney is with Byron."

Clyde taps his desk with a pen.

"With whom?"

I point to the wall behind him.

"The guy who did the painting over there. Pavie. Marcel Pavie."

Clyde loosely crosses his legs, bends back on his chair, rests his hands on his belly, and smiles. A big, broad, satisfied smile.

"Finally!"

"Why, you knew?" I ask.

"Marcel Pavie called here this morning," Bonnie starts.

"And he explained everything," Clyde concludes.

My back, my butt, and my throat tighten. I swallow hard.

"So what's going to happen to me?"

Clyde emits a cavernous laugh.

"Nothing."

"Nothing? So why the charade? All this time you have been playing with me. Is this my lawyer's office or a fucking torture chamber?"

Another grin from Clyde. I look at him. In my head I make a list of animals, trying to decide which one might be able to chop off his kind.

"Nothing is going to happen to you, Zoe," Bonnie explains, "because—"

"Because I am your lawyer," Clyde interrupts, "and because of Mysoul Pawvee—"

"Marcel Pavie," an irritated Bonnie corrects.

Clyde looks at me.

"How do you pronounce his name, Zoe?"

"Byron."

Clyde sends a predatory glance to Bonnie. Bonnie reciprocates. And back. And forth. Again. And again. Ping-Pong. Bonnie and Clyde. Bonnie and Clyde.

Then Clyde opens a golden box, picks out a cigar, goes through all the petting and licking and preparing that makes wives and lovers wish they were cigars themselves.

"Well, let's use Byron, and fuck Mysoul! Ha, ha, ha!" he says between inhales. "Your friend Byron, Zoe, is a very rich man with very rich friends. Even the very powerful Donald Chancecastle can do nothing against Byron and the LA elite who buy his paintings."

"You buy his paintings," I state.

"The painting above—a bit strange, if you ask me, but I know it's very valuable—well, it was a gift."

Am I really a pro bono case? Or has Byron just paid Clyde's fees in advance with one of his masks?

"Then why call you?" I ask. "If Byron and his friends are as powerful as you say—"

"To make our stories coincide, my dear. I mean Zoe."

I massage my forehead.

"Ah, fiction. We're back to fiction. So what is the story?"

"What's the story, Bonnie?"

Bonnie gets up and grabs the file from Clyde's hands. She leafs through it, pulls out a handwritten piece of paper and reads.

"'Donald Chancecastle might have been too saddened by the death of his sister to realize that one of his good friends from Florida, a Felicia Narbum, of the Narbum, Narbum and Curcis legal firm, adopted Barnaby in accordance with the will of Terry Chancecastle. Ms. Narbum, too busy at the time to pick up Barnaby, asked her friend Marcel Pavie to bring her the lynx, since he was already headed to Florida to visit friends. She and Mr. Pavie wish to clear Ms. Zimmerman's name regarding the alleged kidnaping of Barnaby. Facts about the lynx's so-called abduction and Ms. Zimmerman's participation therein have been misconstrued. Barnaby now is very happy in a special space at Ms. Narbum's estate, where he plays with other lynxes. Ms. Narbum will give a press conference from Miami, and Mr. Pavie will also talk to the press in Los Angeles, so the matter of Barnaby's disappearance will be settled once and for all.'"

Clyde sits up, tightens his tie.

"And I, of course, will have a press conference right here in New York."

"And they will believe that? What if they visit Byron's home and see Lord Barney there? What if Donald Chancecastle denies all of this?"

Bonnie bends toward me.

"No chance of that. Ms. Narbum is the key here. First, she is a well-known cat lover. She owns all sorts of felines. When the press sees them, they will assume Barnaby is one of the bunch. Furthermore, Felicia is not, as the statement suggests, a good friend of Mr. Chancecastle. Rather, she is his enemy. A very potent enemy who knows more than a few dirty little secrets about him."

"Donald Chancecastle has...how shall I put it...unusual sexual tastes. And he doesn't want these eccentric habits of his to become public," Clyde adds.

"And what about the real Lord Barney, who is with Byron?"

Clyde lifts his shoulders.

"An eccentric artist who decided to get his own lynx, that's what people will think. Or the cat was a present from Ms. Narbum."

"So that's it? We're done?"

"Oh, no, Zoe! That was just the prologue. Now we get into Terry Chancecastle's murder."

"But I am innocent, dammit! How can anyone believe I could do such a freaky thing?"

Clyde smirks.

"Indeed, let's just tell that to the DA. That will work."

I ignore him.

"And I don't like knives. And even if I were a murderer, why would I kill Terry Chancecastle?"

Sadness hits me like a hammer. Tears come to my eyes. I lower my head and run my index fingers right under the eyeliner. Got to learn to control myself better.

"What's the matter?" Bonnie asks.

I look at her and then at Clyde, who is performing fellatio on his cigar.

"I really liked her."

Clyde huffs and puffs white smoke, producing a nauseous smell. Then he gives a grunt, a cough, both of them preparing him to recite in his melodious voice.

"Some people say you liked her a little too much."

"Actually, it's the other way around," Bonnie says. "People say that Terry Chancecastle liked Zoe a little too much."

Clyde blows smoke in Bonnie's direction. She slaps the air to and fro.

"Well, the photo in her apartment—" she continues.

"Well, the fact that Zoe right here took the liberty of calling her Agatha Christie!" Clyde snaps.

I get up.

"What are you doing?" Clyde demands.

"Leaving! If you two enjoy these little sexual innuendos, go ahead batting them about! And if it turns you on, great! Clyde's desk can fit the biggest fantasies. But me, I'm going. Contrary to its effect on you two, this place does not stimulate my libido. Neither did Terry Chancecastle, by the way. What she stimulated in me was respect and the love of a job well done. And if I called her Agatha Christie, so what? I'll tell you something. She knew the nickname I gave her. It amused her. And I'll tell you something else. At least the real Agatha Christie could work a plot a lot better than you two sex-obsessed Central Park West puppets!"

Bonnie and Clyde look at each other.

"Wow!" Bonnie exclaims after a moment. "Looks like the cognac has been defeated. Remind us to put you on the witness stand."

"Marc told me about you," Clyde comments. "I guess he was right. Now please sit back down. The three of us are going to talk strategy."

When I go back to my chair, Bonnie takes my hand and says, "I have some information that might interest you. About Donald Chancecastle."

I sit still and wait for the punch line.

"He is a champion knife thrower," she ejaculates after half a minute of theatrical silence.

"And he was once a medical student," Clyde says. He left school for reasons of his own, I guess. But he spent enough years there to have a thorough knowledge of human anatomy."

"So it would have been very easy for him to go behind his sister, pretend he needed to see some files in her cabinet and throw a knife at her back," I say.

"Was her desk far from the file cabinet? I mean far enough for someone to throw a knife into her back?" Bonnie asks.

"Agatha...Terry's office was...is very large. And her desk was right in the middle. She wanted to be able to see everything at a glance. She said the arrangement made it easier for her to find books and documents than it would have been had she set the office up otherwise."

Clyde rubs his chin.

"Is that so, Zoe?"

"That's what she said."

Bonnie turns to me, reads the expression on my face.

"You didn't believe her."

"I think the furniture arrangement was for Lord Barney. The cat could get some exercise that way without disturbing files and important memos."

And then it hits me.

"Lord Barney! Of course!"

"Of course what?" Clyde grumbles.

"Well, I can see Donald throwing a knife in his sister's back from a distance. Although I wonder why he didn't just shoot her, if he really wanted to kill his sister—"

"The noise," Clyde retorts.

"He certainly could afford a silencer," I argue.

"Yes he could," Bonnie emphasizes.

"I guess he's not only sexually deviant. The moron is also deviant in his murdering methods," I say. "Throwing a knife, really! But, see, my point is, how does he get out of the office without being attacked? There must be some trace of bites and claw marks somewhere on his body."

"OK, Zoe. But even if that were true, he could say he was bitten by the lynx before then," Clyde reasons.

"You don't understand. Clyde never went into his sister's office. He said he was allergic to cats, so they had meetings in his quarters. I don't think he was so much allergic to cats as he was scared of Lord Barney."

"A lynx, really?" Clyde gives a doubtful frown.

"A fat one with huge teeth," I retort. "It's a good thing he chose to like me, that we got along."

"I see. So if Donald has feline bites on his body—"

Bonnie scratches her chin with her index finger.

"Mm...Interesting."

I wonder if that was the cognac that—after a couple of side effects— helped clarify my mind. Or the coffee. Or Byron's mask above Clyde's head.

I dismiss these possibilities.

It was probably Agatha Christie.

The problem is, how does one tell the police that Donald Chancecastle's butt can be construed as evidence?

22

"We are switching strategies to fight this cancer," Dr. Fontaine tells me.

The man is as plastically altered as ever. And the Grecian Formula got mixed on his head not too long ago. If I remove my glasses, details of his face and hair will disappear, and he will look doable, more or less. Unfortunately, I had a sleepless night and my glasses hide at least partially what my makeup cannot cover. If he saw the rings under my eyes, I am sure he would offer to lend me some Botox. I bet he's saving some in the back room somewhere in case his chin drips or his eye sockets travel south.

"Switching strategies?" I echo.

"We're not going to operate," he states. "Not now, anyway."

Frankly, I find it fascinating the way doctors say "we" when the correct pronoun is obviously "I." Is it because: a) "I" is too small for their inflated egos, so they turn themselves into a duo, or b) They are somewhat cross-eyed and when they see themselves in the mirror, they see double. I'll figure it out later. Right now, I want to rejoice, dance around, and sing that my boob is staying, my boob is staying. But Dr. Fontaine's face is unsmiling.

"We're going to start you on chemo," he says. "I think we want to first reduce the size of the tumor and lymph nodes. You will get four doses of A-C, to be followed by four doses of Taxol, which you will take every three weeks for a total of four doses. But before that, I will give you an anti-inflammatory steroid drug."

I am starting to get a notion of why the "we."

"Why?" I ask.

"To prevent an allergic reaction to the other drugs."

I twist a strand of hair around my finger.

"So I will lose my hair."

"Most probably, yes, Zoe. Some women actually do keep their hair. But those instances are fairly rare."

It's not the man competing with his bright protégé I see today. The affectation that he spread like melted butter on lobster is gone. In front of me, beneath the dyed hair and the swelled face, is a doctor. A genuine doctor.

"I am sorry, Zoe."

He hands me several drug samples.

I get up.

"Do I get a prescription?"

He shakes my hand, gently taps my back.

"These will last until your next time. Ask Claire at the desk to make an appointment."

■ ■ ■

When I get home, Zieg I is sitting on the sofa with a gift in his hands. He hands it to me.

"What's the occasion?" I ask.

"Open it."

"OK, but let me admire the wrapping for a second." One side of the gift paper reaches far into the back of the present; the other side is painfully trying to close at the edge. "Symmetry isn't your thing, is it?" I say, and I think of Hercules Leek, his perfect mustache, and the way he rearranged the objects in Donald's office. "I know a cop who could fix that for you."

"Come on, Zoe!"

I remove the wrapping and find...a book on Tibet.

Zieg watches me turn the pages.

"So you'll think of me when I'm gone."

"You're leaving soon?"

"As soon as they—as the doctor...uh...operates on you."

"Well, I've got news. I'm keepin' my booby."

"Really?"

"But I'm gonna lose my hair."

"Chemo, hey?"

I avoid his glance. Tears come again, uninvited. Before I get a chance to dry them, Zieg comes to hug me.

"Come on, sis. Let's face it, we're both gonna lose our hair."

■ ■ ■

Zieg is sitting on a chair in the middle of the bathroom. I am standing behind him, a pair of scissors in my hands.

"You're sure?" I ask.

"For the hundredth time, yes!"

I let my free hand rub his red curls.

"I'm gonna miss these!"

"I'm not! No more shampooing!"

"You mean, you won't wash your head afterward? Do you plan to grow an insect menagerie up there?"

"Zoe, I'm counting to three until you start using those scissors."

"Count to four and I'll use them on your tongue!"

I start cutting. A few minutes later, I pick up a razor.

When I am done I have trouble recognizing my brother. The surface of his cranium is smooth, like an egg. And so I think, if I opened it, what kind of yolk would I find?

"What's the matter?" Zieg wakes me from my daydream.

"Nothing," I lie.

"Well, can I see?"

"I'm warning you. You won't recognize yourself."

"But it'll look good with a red toga, right?"

"Yeah, even better with high heels and a little mascara."

He gets up, looks at himself in the mirror.

"Boy! My nose really sticks out now! Is that really my face?"

"You're right. You won't know the full effect until you're in full Buddhist attire. Do the monks in Tibet wear hoods?"

Zieg's eyes beg for mercy. He's the child realizing his new toy is not as marvelous as he thought.

"This new look gives you a dignified air," I lie again.

"You think?"

"Absolutely. Plus, imagine, if you monks are out of sand for your sand paintings, you can start making pictures on each other's head!"

He runs his hand across his head.

"Or if you're out of paper, you can start writing your novels on my new hair-free surface!"

"Nay! Your head couldn't handle it."

He makes faces in front of the mirror and then starts laughing. I decide to keep him company. Eventually, my laughter subsides.

Zieg sees my sober expression.

"What now?"

"I need to ask you something, Zieg."

"Sure, sis."

"You know what I just did to you?"

Zieg's face darkens. Obviously he's anticipating what I am going to tell him, and he doesn't like it.

"No!"

"I did it for you! I don't see the problem—"

"I am going to be a Buddhist monk. I need to get used to this."

"And I'm going to go through chemo. I'm going to lose my hair! You said it yourself, we're both gonna lose our hair. Yours is done. Now, do mine!"

"You never know with drugs. Maybe chemo won't destroy your hair."

"You don't want to take the responsibility, is that it?"

"Zoe, that's not fair."

"Oh, no? Tell me what is—fair!"

"You're too upset. You should think about this for a while. You love your hair. Why do you want to get rid of it when you don't know for sure if it's going to fall out?"

"Because I'm not that lucky. It's going to fall out. You know what will happen in a few weeks? I'll brush my hair, and it will stay there—on the brush. And then I'll brush some more, and more will go. Until my head starts looking like an old rug, with most of the hair gone, and just a sick curl hanging here and there. Is that what you want to happen to me? Am I not allowed a little bit of dignity, just because I have cancer?"

I start to cry. Zieg hugs me and cries with me. But then he dries his tears, and I dry mine with my hair.

"Sit down," he finally says.

He cuts one lock and then another, with all the gentleness this big clumsy creature has found within. I suddenly realize that his well is full. Full of that tenderness that, as a man, he has had so few occasions to release. For the first time, I feel that Zieg has made the right decision. A liberating decision, really. Now he can be sensitive, he can be introspective. He can be humble. He can say "fuck you" to Western values—in proper Buddhist language, of course. He can paint on sand, and then offer his art as a gift to the wind. He can be free.

The rhythm of the scissors is steady, rhythmic like a percussion instrument. I keep my eyes closed. I feel like part of my life is being removed with each click of the blades. It's a cleansing feeling. My past is being removed. My mother used to brush the hair of Zoe the little girl in a pitiless way. I used to bite my fingers so as not to cry from the pain. And I think, this is being removed with Zieg's clippers. The way lovers took refuge beneath my hair while they kissed my neck, well, that is being removed. The exclamations of friends or passers-by over my flamboyant mane—that is being removed, too. Terry Chancecastle's fascination with my lion's hair is being removed. Without my hair, I am going to own myself.

Zieg proceeds to the last step. He spreads shaving cream all over my head, fills the sink with fresh warm water, and picks up a razor. His movements are deliberate, attentive, precise. In the end, he applies lotion to where my hair used to be. The massage of a brother over his sister's naked head. I want to tell him to take a pen and draw new maps, new countries, a whole new world, after he is done with the lotion.

When the phone rings, I rush to answer it.

Perhaps not to look at myself in the mirror.

"Hi! Zoe?" the voice asks.

"Mm—" Now that my hair has been deleted, I am in a minimalist mood.

"It's Donald."

I scratch my cranium.

"What do you want with me, Donald? You already fired me! You can't fire me twice!"

"Well, that's what I wanted to talk to you about. I—well, our accountants—ran over the Chancecastle budget. Anyway, to make a long story short, you can come back to your old job if you still want it."

Donald, being nice to me? What's going on?

Can I go back to my old job with a head like this?

23

Today I am going for the Gypsy look. The red dress with the obscene amount of ruffles I am wearing is compensating for the absence of hair.

"You should wear this with your dress."

I am stunned. Now that the guy is switching religions, he's also acquiring the taste of a gay couturier. He has foraged in my scarf basket and found the perfect one to match my dress. I tie it to the back of my head and make the necessary folds and adjustments. The mirror brings to my mind the image of a flamenco dancer with pirate connotations. Carmen meets Long John Silver. Carmen as bald soprano.

"Here," Zieg says as he hands me a pair of hoop earrings.

I put the earrings on and then examine my brother very closely.

"You know, Zieg, there's still time to forget the Buddhist venture, and go into fashion design."

Zieg ignores me. Instead, he brings up Donald's offer.

"You don't have to do this," he says.

"What am I supposed to do, Zieg? If I don't get some Swiss cheese for the rat, he won't talk to me. I could sell myself, but with my hair gone, God knows what kind of clientele I would get."

"I can lend—I can actually give you some money. Where I am going, I won't need much."

"What about Vivian?"

"Fuck Vivian! Let the bitch fend for herself."

"Oh, my little zen-ish Zieg!"

"Vivian makes a six-figure salary. You know that, Zoe."

"What if she loses her job?"

"You've got to be kidding! People are too scared of her to fire her."

"Were you?"

"Don't change the subject, Zoe. This Donald Chancecastle, he's dangerous."

"Indeed. He's a murderer."

"Then why are you going back there? Don't you find it suspicious that he's calling you back, days after firing you?"

"Very."

"Then you are crazy. Or it's the chemo—"

"You don't understand, Zieg. I have to go back."

"To get killed?'

I take my brother's hands, lift my glance to meet his. I am slowly getting used to his unframed features. His bushy looks hid a gentleness that is now fully exposed.

"Listen, I am a murder suspect, and if Donald wants me back, it's probably to frame me."

"Exactly."

"But I have to find out a few things. I know how to frame Donald back, so to speak."

"I think you're nuts. Besides, Chancecastle is already a suspect. The main suspect, I believe. So what are you talking about, Zoe?"

"Well, I know what will make him a bigger suspect yet!"

"Besides greed?"

"Besides greed. Besides his obsession for control. Besides his jealousy over his sister. Besides his ability to throw knives. It's something more tangible, more concrete."

"More concrete? Like what?"

"Lynx bites."

Zieg is still holding my hands, and looking at me intently.

"Excuse me?"

"Lynx bites."

"I knew it! I should never have cut your hair. I must have severed part of your brain."

"You don't get it. When Donald went to kill his sister, her lynx was in her office."

I rearrange my coif.

"It was late," I continue. "Mrs. Beining was probably in bed by then. So, see, there were only three actors in the drama at the time of the crime: Agatha Christie, Donald, and Lord Barney. And Lord Barney is the key to the mystery. Lord Barney, and Donald's butt. Lord Barney won't talk, but Donald's butt can tell a lot of things"

Zieg lets go of my hands.

"Let's assume your view has some validity. I doubt it does, but I'll humor you for a second. So Donald enters his sister's office, kills her, and is immediately attacked by Lord Barney. Now we have Donald's legs and derriere covered with Lord Barney's bites and scratches. Great. But how do you suppose you are ever going to see them, unless Donald decides to wear a miniskirt?"

"Bites and scratches?" I say. "Are you kidding? Do you know how lethal a lynx's bite can be? If that asshole got bit, he probably had to go to the emergency room. Or find an S and M buddy with medical training. An S and M MD. Unless…"

"Unless what?"

"Unless he took care of the wounds himself."

"What are you talking about, Zoe?"

"Well, I heard at the office that Donald went to medical school before he went to work with his sister. He didn't pass the final exams. But still, he would know enough to be able to patch up and disinfect his own butt. No witness, no potential blackmail to take care of. All clean, all secret."

Zieg grabs me by the shoulders, shakes me.

"Stop it!"

"And you know what else? After the murder, Donald walked with a cane for a week or two. Said it was his arthritis, that during difficult times, it came and didn't leave him alone. That with the death of his sister, no painkiller helped. I bet his arthritis was actually Lord Barney's signature on his fat ass."

I pull Zieg's hands off of my shoulders.

"And what about blood? If Lord Barney bit him, there must be blood on the clothes he wore that night."

"There's such a thing called laundry," Zieg retorts.

I give him a smug smile.

"Oh, yeah? Do you really think Donald wears washable clothes? Ralph Lauren, Armani, Dolce and Gabbana, that's what that fuckhead wears. Silks and wools you take to the dry cleaner."

"And do you think he would keep his dirty clothes in his closet as a souvenir, Zoe? He probably threw them away. And, guess what, the cops haven't found them. But, I mean, scavenging in the trash in New York, it's like—"

For some reason, Zieg can't finish his thought. He taps his mouth and lets his eyes wander around the ceiling and back. He then stops the tapping and stares at me.

I look at my watch.

"I have to go."

Zieg helps me on with my coat and grabs his own.

"Let me go with you."

"No."

"Zoe, you're not being reasonable."

"Ha! Look who's talking!"

I see the hurt in his face.

"Why don't you practice a few yoga moves with Zieg II to kill some time?"

He almost smiles.

24

I am five blocks away from the Chancecastle building when I hear a raspy little voice. A woman's voice. At first, I can't make out what she is saying. But she keeps repeating it, like the lines of a lullaby, and the message finally becomes clear.

"Come and see my garden. Come and see my garden."

I look around, see no one. But the voice doesn't stop.

"Come and see. Come, come. Come and see my garden."

I stop, close my eyes for a second, and take a deep, deep breath. I hope it's not some Joan of Arc thing revisiting after six centuries. I don't tend sheep. I don't ride horses. As a woman who only deals with wireless bras and seldom wears pantyhose, I wouldn't be caught dead in a suit of armor. And I hear the British can't cook. So if they toasted me over a campfire, even the wolves would get indigestion.

"Come and see my garden."

I twist my body and look around in all directions, hoping to see something materialize. Nothing.

I am about to get my cell phone out and make an appointment with a psychiatrist when I see her. In a very narrow alley, cutting through the buildings like a vertical abstraction sign, there is a woman standing there. Four feet ten at most, about seventy, all dressed in black and white. Her leggings, sweater, coat, and hat have a zebra pattern—a zebra in need of a bath. Her face reminds me of a photo I saw recently in a literary journal—a portrait of French author Marguerite Duras taken at the end of her life; a tiny woman, disheveled, with eyes that had seen too much and wanted to see more, wearing white socks like a little girl.

Hair sticks out from underneath the Zebra Lady's hat like a dirty cloud. I am not sure it was intelligence I saw in Duras's glance, or simply madness.

"Come and see my garden."

I don't know what makes me follow Madame Zebra down her dark little path, but I do. She walks with quick little steps, like the genuine proprietress of all this narrowness. Fifty yards later, we reach our destination. Fifty yards is a long way when the smell of urine, feces, and garbage accompany your every step.

We come upon a giant cardboard box. The box must once have held a very large sofa. Pot after pot of artificial plants creep over the mildewed roof. Rubber and snake plants for the most part, some standing, some fallen, with leaves missing or broken containers, or both. The entrance of the box is bracketed by two more diseased synthetic plants. The zebra lady smiles a dented smile and tells me to look inside, and to do this I must squat. I gather and lift the ruffles of my dress so they won't come in contact with the ground. Inside the box, a patchwork of old rubber and carpet mats, the ones used in cars, layers the humid floor. A small inflatable mattress and torn blankets eat up most of the space. I get up, meet Madame Zebra's eyes, and attempt a smile. I am afraid I am only able to produce a tight grimace.

Beyond the box a grocery cart rests against the blind wall. A piece of translucent plastic—once a shower curtain, probably—covers an assortment of multicolored, multispotted clothes, shoes, and miscellaneous objects half-buried in the wrinkled mass.

"So do you like my garden?"

There is something ardent in her raspy voice, and in the faded eyes, something like a forgotten light. Crushed between dark walls, mildew and refuse, I have before me Madame Zebra, lady extraordinaire, presenting her paper palace and her field of dreams.

I open my purse. A ten-dollar bill is floating there. I hand it to her. I want to tell her to buy herself some food. But something else comes out of my mouth.

"Here, so you can get some more plants for your...for your garden."

"Oh, thank you, dear. Wait, wait—don't go. I'll give you something. Something you need."

"I don't need anything, ma'am."

That's not what I meant to say, either. But right now, in this forgotten slice of darkness, it rings true. I know the way out. I don't need anything.

"Oh yes, you do." She lets her small quick steps take her to the grocery cart, where she digs through worn-out sweaters, torn coats, spoiled skirts, and dresses of all sizes and, it seems, all historical periods. She digs through tangles of broken belts and pants with shiny bottoms. She pushes aside soleless shoes, damaged boots, and mismatched socks. She roots among little boxes, some wooden and some porcelain boxes, that are chipped or incomplete; she turns up one-armed clocks and dead flowers. Finally, she returns with a costume diadem in one hand and a plastic bag in the other.

She hands me the diadem.

"Put this on top of your scarf, dear, so you will look like a queen."

I look at the little tiara which, miraculously, is clean, and I humor her. "How do I look?"

"Put it more on your left. Yes, like this, like this. Now you look like a queen. Like a queen. Your hair is gone, sweetheart, but now you have a crown. A crown."

She then focuses on the plastic bag.

"Oh, I've got to clean this. Oh, indeed, indeed, I've got to clean this," she whispers. She's focused intently on the bag. For a moment she's a statue. A fragile black-and-white figure with head bent, hands like old roots paralyzed over some object hidden in a supermarket bag. Only the lips move. "Clean this. Got to clean this."

Now her body starts trembling a little. She raises her eyes to the sky. A pale sun hits the ravines in her face. She seems surprised by the light, and her head moves this way and that. Now she lifts her hands to the sky and lets the bag dangle on her arm—a barren Joshua tree with one last leaf stubbornly hanging. She then bends her limbs—so gracefully, like a dancer—to touch her cheeks. She repeats the same act of lifting, lowering, and touching, lifting, lowering, and touching, again and again. I finally understand. She's grabbing the piece of blue sky hanging over the alley; she's grabbing the sun. She's catching a timid warmth and she feels victorious.

But then her head falls over the bag again, and distress returns.

"Got to clean this. Got to clean this."

Obviously her mind has deleted my presence. She is alone, facing what in her world is a major problem.

I hesitate and then tap on her shoulder and say, "Perhaps I can clean it for you."

"Oh, I don't know, dear. It has bad spots. Bad, bad spots."

"Let me see," I ask.

"Oh, but be careful, dear. Be very careful. It has bad spots. Bad spots. Maybe some S.O.S. Have you got some S.O.S.? Yes, S.O.S. is good. It should take off the bad spots. Then it will be clean. Clean. Here, dear, go take off the bad spots, and then bring it back. Yes, bring it back. Bring it back clean."

I open the bag. And then I open my mouth. How long do I stay like this, immobile, aghast? All I know is that, at some point, I let the bag drop. I bend and grab it. Then I lean against the dark wall. I am almost glad to find myself in a cramped alley. The foul assortment of smells and dirt has no grip on me at the moment. Like a surgical cast straightens parts of the body, the narrow alley stabilizes me. It is both uncomfortable and reassuring.

I pick up my cell phone.

The Zebra Lady hits my arm.

"Who you calling, dear? Who you calling?"

I point a finger to the bag I am holding.

"I am calling people who can clean this and remove the bad spots."

I dial the number.

"NYPD," a rugged voice responds.

"Hello! Please connect me to Julie Hoffman."

"What name?"

"Julie Hoffman, I just told you."

"No, your name."

"Zoe."

"Zoe, what?"

"Zimmerman."

"Zoe Zimmerman?!"

"Isn't it what I just said?"

"You're kinda a celebrity, aren't ya?" He chews gum right in my ear before he philosophizes. "Gettin' your fifteen minutes 'n' all that."

Then I hear a few more gum mastications which would offend the most tolerant of cows.

I feel pimples bursting out of my skin. I am really allergic to morons.

"Can you please connect me to Julie Hoffman?"

"OK, OK, I'll transfer ya."

Silence sneaks through, and then macho moron and his chewing return.

"Detective Hoffman ain't…isn't—"

"What can I do for you, Miss Zimmerman?" someone interrupts. This time, the voice is cultured, seemingly out of context. I know right away to whom it belongs. I bet he's petting his mustache and straightening his three-piece suit.

"Detective Leek, you've got to come. You and Julie have got to come here right away."

Leek doesn't ask questions.

"Detective Hoffman stepped out. But I'll find her. I'm on my way. Tell me where you are."

25

For the next fifteen minutes I do my best to entertain Madame Zebra. She starts to get fidgety and wants me to return the bag to her.

"Let's get it cleaned first," I repeat each time she wants to pull it away from me.

She frowns like a child.

"You don't have S.O.S. That's it, you don't have S.O.S. Got to clean it. Got to clean it."

I walk toward the box.

"Let's take care of your beautiful garden." I pick up one pot, straighten it. "Here, see, like this. Let's clean up your garden."

For a moment she gets involved with her broken pots. She picks up an empty sprinkling bottle from her cart and proceeds to do a mock watering of the plants.

My head hurts. I suddenly realize the discomfort is due to the tiara gripping my head through the scarf. I take it off, massage my skull.

The Zebra Lady takes my hand.

"Come and see my garden now. Come and see my garden. Wait. Where is your crown, dear? You have to put your crown on to see my garden. Only queens can see my garden."

I want to tell the lady that it has been a while since I lost my kingdom. But I put my tiara back on. Ouch!

"No, dear. Not like this. Your crown is twisted. Got to be straight, got to be straight. Put it more on the right. Here, let me take the bag from you. Give me the bag, so you can straighten your crown."

I can't help smiling. She's actually trying to distract me—conniving, really—so she can recapture her bag. She looks at me with expectant eyes, hoping her ruse will work.

"Look!" I say. "These two people will get it clean."

Saved by the bell, I think. Or, to be more precise, saved by sirens.

There are two police cars at the end of the alley now, flashing their lights as if it were disco night. As for the siren symphony, I bet that, from the bottom of his grave, Beethoven is at last thankful he is stone deaf.

■ ■ ■

Julie Hoffman walks toward me with an energetic step. She is wearing cargo pants and a leather coat. Her short hair bounces slightly as she walks. She reacts to the stench by twitching her nose like Samantha the Witch. Behind her, Hercules Leek progresses more slowly, looking at every detail of the alley, and holding a handkerchief over his nose and mouth.

■ ■ ■

"What happened to your hair?" Julie remarks as she reaches me.

"I sent my hair to boot camp. It was driving me crazy."

Julie looks at my dress, raises her hands to each side of her head, snaps her fingers, and then shows me the other end of the alley.

"Spain is further that way."

I hand Julie the bag. "OK, but before I go olé-olé or dance flamenco, I thought you might want to see this."

She opens the bag. Detective Leek is now watching over her shoulder.

"A dirty knife," he states.

"Blood stains, looks like," Julie adds.

Wow! Aren't the members of the NYPD a bunch of undeclared geniuses? I reflect.

"Maybe it's the murder weapon."

Julie's hands are now by her belt, her right thumb lightly touching her gun, her eyes traveling up and down, right and left, and then on me.

"Sure, Z-Z." She produces a tight-yet-amused smile. "What murder? This is New York City."

Fuck her! The bitch is making fun of me.

"Why, Julie, the recent murder of Winnie the Pooh!" I explode.

"'Bout time that thing got killed," she replies.

■ ■ ■

From where I sit, at Julie's desk, I can see that the Zebra Lady has taken a real liking to Detective Leek, who is now questioning her a few feet away from us. His hands pet his ballooning stomach. He's wearing a Mona Lisa smile underneath his mustache. Déjà vu, I think.

He has, it seems, the patience of a spider. His green eyes are lit up.

But Madame Zebra has her own reading of Leek. You would think she was at a tea party, joining royalty, as she produces coquettish little gestures in response to Leek's focused interrogation. I am curious to see how he will make her realize that she's not really at Buckingham Palace, that this is not Prince Charles trying to score while Camilla is grabbing some goodies at the other end of the hall.

Julie gets up and returns minutes later with two cups of coffee. During her brief stroll, she has assessed the Leek-Madame Zebra situation. She sends a coded glance to Leek.

"What did you just say to your colleague?" I ask as she hands me my coffee.

"Nothing. Did you see me open my mouth?" Half of her mouth smiles.

Leek gets up from his desk and takes Madame Zebra's arm. Delete the police station decor, add instead a few trees, a lake and some benches, and it's His Roundness and her Tininess promenading on a Sunday afternoon on the island of La Grande Jatte, facing a swell future. Que Seurat, Seurat.

I place my cup on Julie's desk, next to the tiara I have removed on the sly while the Zebra Lady was not looking.

"What's Detective Leek doing?"

"Z-Z, aren't I supposed to do the questioning here?"

I take the tiara from the desk, play with it.

"I get it!"

Julie sits back in her chair, places her hands behind her head.

"You get what?"

"He's trying to get into her world, is that it? He's changing strategies, going where she's going, that is, in her mind, so he can find out where she got the knife."

"You mean, the arm of the crime," Julie teases.

I shrug my shoulders.

"You'll see."

"Well, why don't you put that stuff in one of your novels? Right now, the knife is being analyzed. We'll see whether it killed Terry Chancecastle or someone else. Someone slaughtered a pig, maybe."

I have seen the knife. It could cut Julie's sharp tongue in no time. I try to convey that to her with one of my classified glances. But the bitch just smiles.

"If someone had slaughtered a pig, then Donald Chancecastle would be dead," I retort.

Her smile disappears. Mine resurrects.

She now places her elbows on her desk. Her baby blues study my face.

"I bet you have a theory about what happened."

"I do," I declare. "A damn good one."

"Well, shoot!"

I take my cup, drink.

"Your coffee tastes like shit," I say before I begin.

■ ■ ■

"Ha, ha, ha! Ha, ha, ha, ha!"

Everyone at the station turns toward us. Julie's laughter has not changed. It's as loud now as it was when she was a teenager. It hurts my ears and my pride.

"What's so funny?"

"Your fucking theory. That's what's funny, Detective Zimmerman. You can put that in your fiction as well."

I put my tiara back on, straighten my back.

"I think it holds water."

"OK, let's review your theory." Julie's laugh is still present in her voice. "In order to avoid getting attacked by a lynx, Donald Chancecastle throws a knife into the back of his sister. From a distance. It has been established somehow that the guy is a champion knife thrower. Almost as good at the Great Throwdini."

"Who?"

"The Great Throwdini. David Adamovich, I think his name is."

I look at Julie.

"You know about knife throwers?"

"I used to play with them until I became a cop. Now I play with guns."

I give her a twisted grin, no charge.

"Funny. You should work for David Letterman." After a moment of silence between us, I add, "You still haven't told me what's wrong with my theory."

"Z-Z! First, do you really think that, if Chancecastle wanted to kill his sister, he would take such a risk?"

"But he's a champion thrower!"

"Even champion throwers miss their targets once in a while. I am pretty sure that, if indeed he did it, he wouldn't have wanted to take that chance."

"But the knife. I saw it. It's no ordinary shape. The blade, it's like a long leaf. Sharp on both sides."

"Granted, Z-Z, it's meant for knife-throwing."

"So?"

"So here we are. Chancecastle throws a knife into the back of his sister. His knowledge of anatomy allows him to target the perfect spot to kill her instantly. In the process, he avoids being attacked by a lynx, we've established that. But there is a problem—"

"What?" I interrupt.

"The knife. It was not there when we found the body. Someone had to get it. That is, get close to the body and risk being attacked by the big cat."

Neither of us says anything for a moment. She breaks the silence.

"Of course," she says, "the incentive would be to get rid of the evidence."

"Ha! You see?"

Julie shakes her head.

"Wouldn't it be easier to take that risk while stabbing the person right there, up close and personal, and then remove the knife on the spot and leave? Not to mention that the victim would hemorrhage, and thus die faster. On top of that, it would save one trip for our killer. Plus the knife is in his hand now, and he can kill the lynx if it comes at him."

"I suppose," I say grudgingly.

"Oh, and another thing. The angle of the stabbing. Very precise, very methodical. Could not have been done from a distance. The autopsy of Terry Chancecastle's body has determined that. So I want to ask you a question, Z-Z."

Silence.

"What is a cat's primary activity?"

"Well, it's not accounting," I retort. "And it's not asking stupid questions."

"Sleeping, Z-Z. A cat's primary activity is sleeping."

My tiara falls. It lays on the not-so-clean floor like an irrelevant detail. It is with the most alert of steps that a cop walks to the donut room and crushes it on the way.

"So," I finally state, "what you're saying is that Donald Chancecastle took advantage of Lord Barney's sleep to kill his sister."

"That would hold, don't you think?"

I don't want to argue with Julie. I feel tired, very tired all of a sudden. And I wonder, would Lord Barney let Donald get close to Terry? Wouldn't the smell of the bastard wake him up? How deep is the sleep of lynxes anyway?

"There's only one other theory that would hold as well," Julie continues. She reaches her arms up over her head, gives herself a stretch, and stretches the silence between us in the process.

Finally I ask her, "What's that other theory?"

"That someone very familiar with Barnaby committed the crime. Someone the cat would never think of attacking. Someone like you, Zoe Zimmerman."

26

I lie on the sofa, my hand like a dead branch over a writing pad. All around me, wrinkled pieces of paper layer the floor like snowballs. The pen won't word what I need to word. Letter, ink, stamp, it has become passé, hasn't it? Mailboxes with their big hollow mouths used to swallow it all: impeccable calligraphy, impossible scribbles, announcements that little Roger got a new bicycle and new stitches on his knees, that Grandma Patty went to the beyond toothless but with a grin on her face and that big diamond ring that everyone wanted, that the young blonde living with Old Bill is not really his niece. All that mailboxes eat up now is junk, bills, and manuscripts.

Perhaps I should send him an e-mail.

Or give him a call.

Or meet him at some café, on neutral ground. And tell him, just tell him.

"Hey, Zoe! You want to hear this?" Zieg yells from the kitchen.

I hear page-leafing sounds. From where I lie, they sound like the crackles of a young fire mixed with whispers. I also hear something new in Zieg's trombone voice—a little flute, gliding soft and serene. The Himalayas are getting closer, and my brother is ready to climb. His suitcase sits by the door.

"Hear what?" I mumble.

I know he can't hear me. And so he will come, big and bald, his face like the sun, lines curling upward at the corners of his eyes.

He's here now, tabloid in hand. He looks at the balls of paper all over the rug.

"You're busy redecorating? I thought rejection slips went on the bathroom wall."

I sit up.

"Not this type of rejection slip. I'm the author of the rejection this time."

"And you're sending it—where?"

I pick up a ball, throw it at Zieg. I miss my target.

"To you for being such a nosy prick." I attempt a smile.

"You missed."

I reach for his hand.

"Come, sit here and read me your damn article."

Zieg makes himself comfortable on the sofa. He takes my feet, puts them on his lap, and opens the paper.

"It's from the *Enquirer.*"

"I don't want to know!" I throw another paper ball at him, and this time, it stays on his head like a silly pompon. "You read that shit now?"

"Last temptation before I leave." The paper ball falls between his legs. He looks at it. "I already have two of these I won't need anymore. I really don't want a third."

"Lovely image," I say.

He puts the ball back on his head and then in the middle of his forehead.

"How is that for a third eye?"

"Let it be, and read your junk," I tell him.

"'Zebra Lady Solves Murder,'" Zieg reads. "'Clarissa Casanova, also known as the Zebra Lady or Madame Zebra, was instrumental in solving the murder of Chancecastle Publishing (CP) CEO Terry Chancecastle. That is what Zoe Zimmerman has been maintaining, to the dismay of Hercules Leek and Julie Hoffman, the two NYPD detectives in charge of the investigation.'"

Zieg stops reading, looks at me.

"Since when do you talk to the tabloids?"

I shrug my shoulders.

"Since when do they need me to write their junk?" I don't have the *New York Times* at hand to hit his head, so I get brave and use my bare hand. "Go on."

Zieg massages the top of his head and continues.

"'Zimmerman, an aspiring author and former Chancecastle Publishing employee, was one of the suspects in the murder until circumstances brought her into contact with Clarissa Casanova, an elderly homeless woman Zimmerman nicknamed the Zebra Lady slash Madame Zebra when she observed that the old woman was dressed entirely in black-and-white clothing with a zebra print. Both nicknames have since been used by NYPD personnel to designate Casanova. Officer Charles Echeverry, who was part of the backup when Leek and Hoffman answered Zimmerman's call, told the *Enquirer* that the alley in which Casanova was residing was 'nearly invisible' and that, although he is a New York native, he 'didn't even know it was there.' As a consequence, it took additional critical minutes for the police to respond to the call that Zimmerman made when she saw that Casanova had a suspicious knife in her possession.

"'Less than a week earlier, Zimmerman had been let go by CP, where she had been employed as an associate editor. However, shortly after being laid off, Donald Chancecastle, Terry Chancecastle's brother, contacted Zimmerman to let her know that the position was hers again if she wanted it. She was walking to work when she heard Casanova calling to her from an alleyway. Zimmerman followed Casanova down the alley, where the elderly woman was residing in a large cardboard box.

"'When Casanova showed Zimmerman a blood-spotted knife, Zimmerman immediately contacted the police and talked to Detective Hercules Leek, who shortly thereafter arrived on the scene with his partner, Detective Julie Hoffman. The knife was sent to a forensics lab for examination. DNA analysis showed that the blood on the blade belonged to Terry Chancecastle and that the fingerprints on the knife's handle belonged to Donald Chancecastle. The forensics findings led to Mr. Chancecastle's arrest.

"'Experts disagree as to how the murder happened. Some assert that Chancecastle, who was once a champion knife thrower, threw the knife into his sister's back. Others affirm Chancecastle stabbed his sister to death with the knife. Chancecastle, who occupies the starring role in what promises to be the trial of the century, refuses to humor the murder theorists one way or the other. All he will say is that he was tired of being number two at CP. He added that he had always known of more effective ways to lead the company, but that his sister had consistently rejected his suggestions. According to Donald Chancecastle, the company needed to downsize and cut employees benefits, but Terry Chancecastle refused to agree to make these changes.

"'Other factors are sure to generate interest in the upcoming trial. One factor concerns Terry Chancecastle's will. In it, she specifies that should anything happen to her, Donald Chancecastle must not be allowed to assume the leadership of CP.'"

"Sounds like Lenin's political will," I interrupt. "'Absolutely no Stalin,' it basically said. Same shit with Hindenburg. No Hitler at the head of the nation, he recommended. And yet look what happened."

Zieg rolls up the *Enquirer*, thwacks my head with it.

I'll have to sue him for plagiarism.

Zieg unrolls the tabloid and finds his spot.

"'Terry Chancecastle's will…' Blah, blah, blah…OK, here we are. 'Terry Chancecastle wanted CP to become an employee-owned company, and to achieve that end she had devised a plan that would enable employees to purchase company shares. During a press conference, New York attorney Clyde Trenton indicated that the will that designated Donald Chancecastle as the successor CEO of CP was a false document.

"'Another element that will be sure to generate interest in the trial is the revelation of Donald Chancecastle's unique personal tastes. It appears that he is as much an S and M expert as he is a knife-throwing expert. He is a member of several select New York S and M clubs, including the Kics Gramos Society, the Frusef and Neyjo Assembly, and the über-exclusive

OuchAndYummy Club. The *Enquirer* promises to further investigate Donald Chancecastle's S and M activities.

"'Zimmerman was asked if she knew that Donald Chancecastle was a dangerous man, and if she did, why was she on her way to work that fateful day when she met the Zebra Woman. She answered that she was convinced that Chancecastle wanted to frame her for the murder of his sister, and that she went to 'frame the framer.' At the time, Zimmerman was convinced that what would save her would be bite marks. Terry Chancecastle had a pet lynx named Barnaby, and apparently, the cat hated Donald. Zimmerman suspected that the cat had attacked Donald when it saw him murder his sister. She felt that if she could produce evidence proving that such an attack took place, the real murderer would be apprehended and her good name would be cleared. 'She took a camera to work with her. She wanted to hide in the men's restroom and take a picture of Donald's bare bottom at the right moment. She planned to show the photo to the police,' a friend of Zimmerman's told the *Enquirer*. The friend wishes to remain anonymous, and Zimmerman will not confirm or deny the veracity of the friend's statements.'"

Zieg scrutinizes me for a moment.

"Is that really what you planned to do? Take pictures of Donald's ass? Look at me, Zoe, and tell me it's not true."

"Zimmerman will not confirm or deny these statements," I say while examining my feet.

Zieg rolls his eyes.

"Is that the end of the article?" I ask.

"No."

"Then what are you waiting for?"

Zieg rolls his eyes once more.

"Stop rolling your eyes. You're not a planet." I tell him.

Zieg scratches his throat and tightens his hold on the *Enquirer*.

"'Bite and scratch marks have since been found on Donald Chancecastle's body, and expert zoologists and veterinarians have identified the marks as having been made by a large-size feline.'"

"Ha!" I interrupt.

Zieg scratches his throat.

"'Whether the marks were caused by Barnaby is hard to determine. Chancecastle did not check into a hospital. Yet the wounds had been medically treated. Some suspect that Chancecastle, who attended medical school but did not pass the final examinations to actually become an MD, treated the injuries himself.

"'But it was the Zebra Lady who was able to concretely connect Donald Chancecastle to the murder of his sister. With the help of police and city government, she was placed in a home from which she has recently disappeared. However, the *Enquirer* has found Casanova again in her old invisible alley. She explained that she needed to return to her home to water her garden.'"

■ ■ ■

Zieg looks at me as if he is going to ask me a few choice questions, but in the end he just puts down the *Enquirer* and says, "I need a glass of water." He looks at his watch. "A quick one."

"Is it time already?"

Zieg gently moves my feet from his lap.

"If I don't go now, I'll miss my flight."

"Let me get you your water."

"Don't move, Zoe. You must rest—with your chemo and all."

I get up, beat him to the kitchen, and hand him his water.

"It's the last favor I'm going to do for you for a long time."

My body shakes, and I try very hard to stabilize it.

Zieg puts his glass on the counter.

"You OK?"

"Fine. Don't worry about it."

"You're not going to cry, are you?"

"If I do, it will be tears of joy. I can finally get rid of you."

Zieg smiles and hugs me hard.

"Bye, sis."

"Don't forget what I told you about hailing a cab. Step on the curb and—"

"We should have called Aimé."

I pray Aimé will be busy elsewhere.

"This is New York. Cabs come by as often and as fast as ants on a pile of sugar."

We look at each other for a moment.

"I can go down with you and hail you a cab if you want," I add.

"I can take care of myself, Zoe. Besides, you're tired."

I hate good-byes.

Zieg gives me another hug, pets my hairless head, and picks up his suitcase.

And then he goes.

I lean my head against the door. How long I stay like this, pressed up against the cold metal, I don't know. I just know I'll miss my monk.

There is a faint crinkling sound coming from the living room.

I look around. I look up. Nothing.

I look down. Zieg II is turning my paper snowballs into tiny snowflakes.

Time to feed a rat.

27

"No. Don't come to my place," I tell him on the phone. "Let's meet at the MoMA. The Pavie exhibit."

■ ■ ■

Byron's African masks surround me. Their angry, astounded, or expectant expressions surround me. A whole continent surrounds me. And he's there in the middle, a dark Adonis, impossibly appetizing. He sees me, rushes toward me. Hugs me. I shouldn't have let him. Now I feel his tight, lithe body, his powerful hold. I feel his hardness. The temptation to start again assails me. His smell of pepper and cinnamon assails me, weakening my knees.

"Why the letter, Z-Z?"

"I thought it would be easier. I thought that a Parisian from Guadeloupe would prefer a letter."

"Any letter from you, Z-Z. Any letter, except a letter like this one."

"Dammit, Aimé! Don't make it harder than it is! Look at me, just look at me!"

"I am looking, Z-Z."

His voice is an even-waved sea, a long stretch of velvet. I shouldn't have come.

"Well, what do you see? Eh, what do you see?"

"The woman I love, that's what I see."

I take his hand, lead him to the painting of a long mask with a wide open mouth. Pavie's version of Munch's *The Scream*.

"Look at it, Aimé. That's me. That's me right now."

"You're prettier than that, Z-Z."

"No, I am not."

Behind his tender gaze I see a touch of pity and it kills me.

"You are beautiful. You will be…beautiful again. Your hair will grow back."

"But now, Aimé, now! You're not ready for this."

"But I can…I can make myself ready."

"You can make yourself ready for another, Aimé. Another woman, with less history and a lot more hair."

"Is that what you think I am after? Appearances? Just appearances?"

"You should be after someone younger. You told me once after making love that you would like children one day. Remember? Well, I can't give you children, Aimé. I can't even give you sex. I'm too exhausted. And you're this vibrant young man, this gift, really, who came and gave me comfort and joy at a time when I really, really needed it."

He kisses my hands.

"You need that now, Z-Z."

I let go of his hands.

"I will always remember what you gave me. And I will never forget you."

We look at each other, two trees after a storm, for a long, long time. His branches are reaching toward the sun. Mine are in need of pruning. Silence glides between us, better than an adieu. Then cold air seems to breeze through the gallery, and I shiver. He bends toward me, takes me in his arms, gives me a long passionate kiss. For one brief moment, I think it is all right, that things can stay the way they are. This man feels so good against me. We are at the very center of the gallery, surrounded by the masks. Visitors start applauding. Do they think that this tall, gorgeous brown man and this white woman with no hair and lots of jewels are part of the exhibit?

Suddenly, Aimé turns away from me and from the masks, and walks toward the exit. Then he comes back to me. He kisses me long and hard once more.

"No, you won't, Z-Z. You won't forget me. And you know why? Because Aimé will be back. Yes, Aimé will be back."

And then, like a restive race horse, he leaves the building.

■ ■ ■

I suddenly remember that last time I was here, I gave the finger to the masks. They had their problems, I had mine. Now I visit each one of them and apologize.

28

Zieg's money has come in handy, and I am grateful for it. I didn't really have my fifteen minutes of fame. Clyde Trenton mobilized the media to make himself the hero of a drama in which he had, in fact, a very minor role. I guess he's ready for politics.

Some publishers contacted me. They wanted me to write an account of the Chancecastle experience. I prefer to rearrange things into fiction, I told them, because fiction makes more sense. They hung up. Something tells me they will call back and that, when they do, I may give them more attention. Perhaps I could write an account that reads like fiction. Capote did the *In Cold Blood* thing, and Grisham did it in *The Innocent Man*. I bet I can do my own thing in my own book.

Lord Barney and Byron made the cover of *Vanity Fair*. The Pavie profile, written by none other than Jane Wolcox, includes that now-famous photo of me taken by Agatha Christie. Hairy lions, hairy Zoe; it's hard for me to look at it now. But it is soothing to read what Byron, ever the gentleman, has to say about his friend Z-Z. Chancecastle Publishing, now an employee-owned company, has called me back. I told them I have trouble concentrating. I might mix up a gardening book with a chick-lit novel, and what would we have then, a sassy woman planting tomatoes? Sounds like Miss Marple, they retorted.

I am quite incapable of doing any mildly demanding physical task. Cleaning the apartment has become a challenge. Walking a few steps to buy croissants or Swiss cheese for Zieg II has become strenuous. I still shave my head, but even that I don't have to do as often as before. There are some strangely cozy, almost comforting moments in disease, at least for a writer. I live in another world, not a dynamic world, not a world of incessant movement, but a world of fatigue and medication, a fuzzed world of meditation. Still, I feel a power coming from within me, an absurd yet real sense of victory. What if my disease were a cleansing, a way to create the perfect tabula rasa, to start over? For some reason, the sun piercing through the window does not bring the same light when one is sick, but it is just as beautiful. It comes to me like the foggy light in a Turner painting. And that's enough for me now. Enough to write every day, sometimes for just half an hour, sometimes for forty-five minutes. Rarely can I last more than an hour. But today, I just finished revising my novel. And tomorrow, I'll craft my best query letter. And the day after, I'll start stuffing envelopes, sending them to agents, to a publisher or two…maybe even to Chancecastle. Why not, after all? In any case, the bottom line is that tomorrow I will start again. Right now I need to rest.

I am about to let myself go to sleep when I hear something. A knock? A knock on the door?

Going by Zieggy's sudden retreat to his hiding place, yes, someone is knocking.

I force my body to rise. I drag my feet to the door.

Boom. Boom. Boom. Three more knocks resound on the door. Almost like at the theater. Announcing what kind of play?

Sometimes crossing this shoebox of a place is like crossing the Sahara. *Boom. Boom.*

I am there now, out of breath. I lean against the door for a moment and then open it. And then I see. I see that his beard has not been meticulously trimmed. That's a first. I see that his glasses are not dust-free like they used to be. I see that the suitcase by his side is not small and carefully packed for just a few days. No, this bag is big and swollen, has been packed in a rush, or in a moment of impossible abandon. This bag is pregnant.

I see lines around the mouth, rings under the deep-blue gaze. I see a face undone. That beautiful Che Guevara face, abandoned. I see the face I have been waiting for.

I don't see him holding a large bouquet of roses from Mr. Liu's flower shop. And I think—damn!—the vase I have been keeping just in case will have to wait.

I see him holding a large chunk of Swiss cheese.

And so I turn around, and I gather all the energy I can muster, and from the depth of my throat, at the point where laughter and tears collide, I call, "Zieg II! Zieg! Oh, Zieggy! Where are you? Come here! Come, my love! Come, come, my rat! You have a visitor!"

ABOUT THE AUTHOR

Marie-Jo Fortis is the author of the critically acclaimed *Chainsaw Jane*. If you want to know more on Marie-Jo, pay her a little visit on www.mariejofortis.com.

www.ingramcontent.com/pod-product-compliance
Lightning Source LLC
Chambersburg PA
CBHW051918240626
47153CB00004B/1274